The DOUCHE JOURNALS

{VOLUME ONE: 2005 – 2010}

THE DEFINITIVE ACCOUNT OF ONE MAN'S GENIUS

Compiled and Annotated by

Schmidt

Foreword by Nick Miller

itbooks
AN IMPRINT OF HARPERCOLLINSPUBLISHERS

Photos on page 9: (left) © George Daniell/Getty Images and (right) © Eastcott Momatiuk/Getty Images. Photo on page 26: © J. Vespa/Getty Images. Illustration on page 70 by Melissa Boock.

itbooks

HarperCollins books may be purchased for educational, business, or sales promotional use. For information please write: Special Markets Department, HarperCollins Publishers, 10 East 53rd Street, New York, NY 10022.

Additional photography courtesy of Patrick McElhenney.

FIRST EDITION

Library of Congress Cataloging-in-Publication Data is available upon request.

ISBN 978-0-06-223867-2

12 13 14 15 16 DIX/RRD 10 9 8 7 6 5 4 3 2 1

The DOUCHE JOURNALS

PREFACE

This book is a journey. Not only for you, the reader, but also for me, as I find myself in the unique position of being both subject and curator. First though, a little history: *The Douche Journals* date back to early 2005, a time in which my body and mind were undergoing rapid transformation. It may be hard for you to imagine now, but as recently as May Day, 2004, I had a body mass index north of 40 and gaps in my pop culture knowledge that you could lead a peloton through. So the metamorphosis began; for six months I lived on a strict diet of meal-replacement shakes and E! Network television. What came out of that chrysalis is the man you see now: taut, sculpted, and conversant in the idiosyncrasies of food, fashion, beauty, doin' it, and the arts.

The Douche Journals grew out of these developments. Like a teenager who grows ten inches in one summer, I suddenly found myself with a surfeit of strength, sexual appeal and sweet, tight game. My roommates were naturally threatened, and instituted The Douchebag Jar (née The Douchebag Bowl, née The Douchebag Saucer) as a way of curbing what they considered to be my more self-destructive tendencies. While I didn't (and don't) always agree with my roommates' judgment concerning douche dos and douche don'ts, I recognize the need for humility and have grown to appreciate the jar as a useful foil in my relentless pursuit of self-perfection, shorties, and money.

What follows is a written record of each (alleged) incidence of doucheness from 2005 to 2010. After putting money in the jar, I took pains to log both the infraction itself and the circumstances surrounding said infraction. However, due to the subjectivity of what does and doesn't fall under douche jurisdiction, this journal should be considered a contested document; it is a piece of history that, like a prism, casts different colors when held up to different lights. It doesn't take too much imagination to conceive of a time when my exploits and aphorisms will be deemed visionary, and my payments to the jar a martyr's sacrifice.

At the same time, this book is also a love story.

I hope you'll find these pages as enlightening, instructive, amusing, subversive, challenging, uncompromising, and morally charged as I have. My words, though at times they cannot manage it, are an ongoing attempt to make palpable the awesome cosmic emptiness through which we all float and fight and love and die.

S.

Coronado Island

June 2012

FOREWORD TO THE FIRST EDITION

by Nick Miller*

Date: 6/8/12

Time: 8:03 PM

To: nmiller34@aol.com

From: thebigs@me.com

Subject: Foreword to Douche Journal Vol. 1

Nick—As you may or may not know, my journals are soon to be published. Pending what I imagine will be universal acclaim, the Second, Third, and Fourth editions will most likely feature forewords by world leaders, both political and spiritual. However, since you instituted the fated Jar in the first place, I feel it is only appropriate to bestow on you the honor of writing the Foreword to the First edition.

That's right. Pick your jaw up off the floor. And start typing!

What I'm hoping you can provide is some context for both the Douchebag Jar's origins and the ways in which it has evolved. The tone should be light, conversational, but learned. Please don't overreach. I cannot emphasize this enough. There's no reason to use a fifty-dollar word when a ten-cent word will do.

---

*Via E-mail

And speaking of words, you have about eighty, so make them count.

We stand at the precipice of publishing history. Will you hold my hand on the way down?

S

Date: 6/24/12
Time: 2:14 AM
To: thebigs@me.com
From: nmiller34@aol.com
Subject: Re: Foreword to Douche Journal Vol. 1

no

Date: 6/24/12
Time: 2:17 AM
To: nmiller34@aol.com
From: thebigs@me.com
Subject: Re: Re: Foreword to Douche Journal Vol. 1

First of all, thank you for responding.

I understand that a responsibility of this magnitude can seem onerous, and I appreciate your humility in the face of such a daunting challenge.

Let me put your fears to rest: you cannot disappoint me.

The publisher has a small army of editors and copyeditors that can take whatever tangled mess of prose you spit out and smooth it into a cogent celebration of my words. There's no need to worry about embarrassing yourself or, more importantly, me.

Having alleviated what I suspect are your fears, I will leave you to it. Create!

S

Date: 6/29/12

Time: 10:42 AM

To: thebigs@me.com

From: nmiller34@aol.com

Subject: Re: Re: Re: Foreword to Douche Journal Vol. 1

leave me alone schmidt

Date: 6/29/12

Time: 11:15 AM

To: nmiller34@aol.com

From: thebigs@me.com

Subject: Re: Re: Re: Re: Foreword to Douche Journal Vol. 1

Nick, I want you to take a long look in the mirror and ask yourself one question: "Why am I afraid of success?"

Date: 7/1/12

Time: 1:41 AM

To: thebigs@me.com

From: nmiller34@aol.com

Subject: Re: Re: Re: Re: Re: Foreword to Douche Journal Vol. 1

can't. busy.

also, not sure yet how much money you're going to have to put in the jar for publishing this book about the jar, but it's going to be a lot. Maybe three digits. Just a heads-up.

Date: 7/1/12

Time: 1:43 AM

To: nmiller34@aol.com

From: thebigs@me.com

Subject: Re: Re: Re: Re: Re: Re: Foreword to Douche Journal Vol. 1

What if I just write something myself and you can sign your name?

Date: 7/1/12

Time: 1:43 AM

To: thebigs@me.com

From: nmiller34@aol.com

Subject: OUT OF OFFICE REPLY: Re: Foreword to Douche Journal Vol. 1

I will be out of the office indefinitely on personal business. Best—NM

Date: 7/2/12

Time: 8:13 AM

To: nmiller34@aol.com

From: thebigs@me.com

Subject: Re: OUT OF OFFICE REPLY: Re: Foreword to Douche Journal Vol. 1

I know you're not out of the office! You don't even have an office, big guy!

Date: 7/2/12

Time: 8:13 AM

To: thebigs@me.com

From: nmiller34@aol.com

Subject: OUT OF OFFICE REPLY: Re: OUT OF OFFICE REPLY: Re: Foreword to Douche Journal Vol. 1

I will be out of the office indefinitely on personal business. Best—NM

2005

Wanderings

■ ■ ■

TOTAL INFRACTIONS: 27
TOTAL AMOUNT: $381

January 1, 2005

"If your annual moisturizer budget doesn't contain a comma then you're doing it wrong."

■ ■ ■

Location: Front door.

Occasion: Triumphant return from Sephora.

Amount: $5 USD.

Notes: Why would I put money in a jar??? Jars are for jellies!

"Thread count is red herring numero uno in 'The Case of the Perfect Bed Sheet.' "

■ ■ ■

Location: Macy's.

Occasion: After a valiant half-decade struggle, Nick's sheets officially disintegrate.

Amount: $18 USD.

Notes: Unfortunately, Nick made his purchase and left the store without hearing:

{ "The 10 questions I always ask *BEFORE* 'What's the thread count?' " }

1. Do these sheets say "seduction" in the evening, "comfort" in the night, and "reassurance" in the morning?
2. Do these sheets possess the will and the crispness to produce razor-sharp hospital corners?
3. Are these sheets champagne-resistant?
4. Do these sheets accurately capture my permanent essence, while allowing for the temporary essence of others?
5. When I'm ready to expand, what will my sham and dust ruffle options be?
6. Will these sheets adequately camouflage the end result of a moderate-to-severe wet dream?
7. Will these sheets draw the eye towards or away from my bed skirt?
8. Are these sheets the most expensive sheets in the store, and if not, why?
9. Will these sheets feel soft to the touch, yet still provide the friction necessary to keep all parties involved from sliding willy-nilly into my scrimshaw headboard?
10. Were these sheets made in the USA?

INFRACTION 3

January 22, 2005

"Sous-chefs be dicing up in here!"

■ ■ ■

Location: 3-star restaurant.

Occasion: Kitchen tour purchased at charity auction, shared by viciously ungrateful "+1" (Winston).

Amount: $22 USD.

Notes: Why would you wave a knife at someone who is only trying to celebrate you?

"I don't dress for the job I have. I don't dress for the job I want. I dress for the job some kid at Stanford is inventing right now."

■ ■ ■

Location: Mirror.

Occasion: Practicing triple Windsor.

Amount: $9 USD.

Notes: If I didn't practice tying ties on Nick, how would I improve?

February 3, 2005

"Who stole my prescription Oakleys? Wait, never mind, they're on the back of my neck."

■ ■ ■

Location: Front door.

Occasion: Bike ride.

Amount: $11 USD.

Notes: Funny story: What I felt on the back of my neck was just my popped collar—Rx Oaks were still in their belt case! What a world.

"Calling a pant 'tapered' is like calling baby food 'nonpoisonous.' It shouldn't have to be said."

■ ■ ■

Location: Customer Service Counter, Nordstrom Rack.

Occasion: Saturday.

Amount: $14 USD.

Notes: Here's what "The Boot Cut Lobby" doesn't want you to know:

There is nothing
more **Anti-Boot**
than the **Boot Cut.**

If you really cared about your boots,
you wouldn't cover them up with extra fabric.

March 17, 2005

"Human Growth Hormone sounds redundant, but I would inject the hell out of some Puma Growth Hormone."

■ ■ ■

Location: Couch.

Occasion: Congressional hearing on steroids.

Amount: $3 USD.

"Is it just me, or does looking at Audrey Hepburn kinda make you want to french kiss a deer?"

■ ■ ■

Location: Movie theater.

Occasion: Midnight *My Fair Lady* with Nick. I can't prove it, but I'm pretty sure he smoked some marijuana beforehand.

Amount: $35 USD.

Notes: Every red-blooded man has thought about it. Put that deer in a pixie cut and you're watching *Roman Holiday*.

May 11, 2005

"First rule of fashion: Only professional athletes may wear olive."

■ ■ ■

Location: Hugo Boss outlet.

Occasion: Deals deals deals.

Amount: $10 USD.

Notes:

★ Second rule of fashion?

The perfect pair of sport sandals is not owning sport sandals.

★ Third rule of fashion?

If it doesn't need to be washed by hand, throw it in the trash.

★ Fourth rule of fashion?

It's not about the wristwatch, it's about the man wearing a better wristwatch than your crappy wristwatch.

★ Fifth rule of fashion?

If your wardrobe were a deck of cards, the jokers would be suede.

★ Sixth rule of fashion?

One day people will talk about Dwayne Wade's cardigans the way we talk about Thomas Edison's light bulb.

★ Seventh rule of fashion?

Besides bearing children, ironing is the noblest thing we do as human beings.

★ Eighth rule of fashion?

Wrinkle-free shirts lack character and contain asbestos.

★ Ninth rule of fashion?

Plum is a viable sweater color every 11 ½ years. Seriously, it's how they set the atomic clock.

★ Tenth rule of fashion?

One percent of your adjusted gross income should go straight to hosiery.

★ Eleventh rule of fashion?

Men who tan quality leathers should be paid more than doctors.

★ Twelfth rule of fashion?

Merino wool is the biggest scam since the South Sea Bubble.

★ The penultimate rule of fashion?

Always match your belt with your attitude.

★ The final rule of fashion?

Have fun!

May 20, 2005

"You can lead a horse to water, but you can't make it dressage."

■ ■ ■

Location: Goldfish bowl.

Occasion: Lord Bubblington's refusal to swim in his Gothic undersea castle home.

Amount: $9 USD.

Notes: Goldfish? More like *PLATINUM* fish! L-Bubs is a baller and the only thing that really understands me.

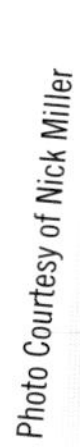

■ ■ ■

Amount: $7 USD.

Notes: The free crepes is the sweetest crepes.

June 23, 2005

"Pubic hair is like a prison population—turn your back for a second, and it becomes unruly."

■ ■ ■

Location: Shower.

Occasion: Bi-Weekly trim.

Amount: $15 USD.

Notes:

{ MY PUBIC HAIR:
A Fond Look Back (Or Down! HAHAHA!) }

TIME PERIOD	PUBIC HAIR STYLE	WORLD EVENTS
1994	On a barren planet, life stirs . . .	Kurt Cobain, RIP.
1994–1996	Healthy Parsley Patch	Million Man March, the DVD, O.J. Simpson Trial
1996–1999	Full Headbanger	Mike Tyson bites ear, Lewinsky scandal
1999–2001	My Secret Garden	Last "Peanuts" comic runs
2002	Crop circles	Dot-com bubble
April 2003	A brief exploration of geometric shapes	Human Genome Project completed
2004	N/A	Gmail launch, Red Sox win World series
Early 2005	The Bowtie: 'cause what I got ain't "*SEMI*-formal . . ."	Prince Charles weds Camilla Bowles

July 4, 2005

INFRACTION 13

"You call this a clambake?"

■ ■ ■

Location: Beach.

Occasion: If not the Chernobyl of outdoor seafood-steaming/eating events, then surely the Three Mile Island. Get organized or don't invite me.

Amount: $10 USD + $8 USD = $18 USD.

Notes: This would've just been a tenner, but I was wearing my Nantucket Reds when I said it.

INFRACTION 14

July 28, 2005

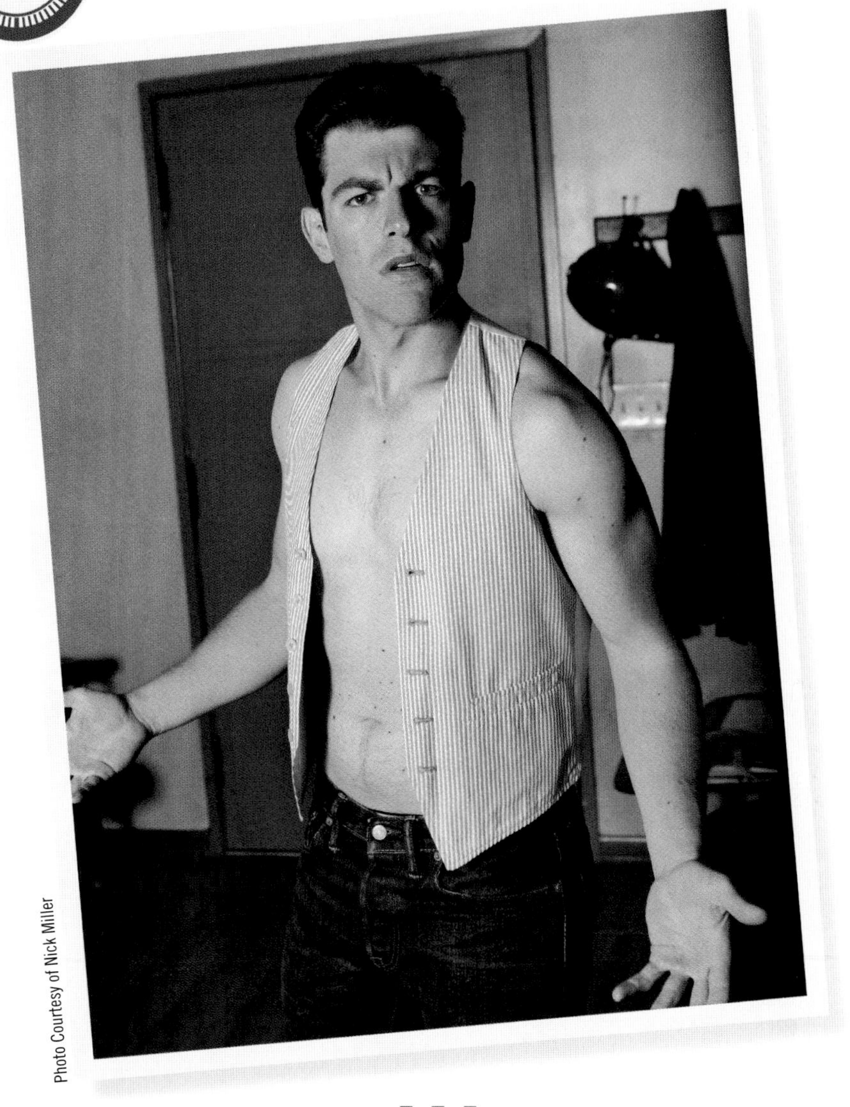

Photo Courtesy of Nick Miller

■ ■ ■

Amount: $11 USD.

Notes: What?! My hat and cane are in the car.

"One man's topography is another man's PORNography."

■ ■ ■

Location: Winston's car.

Occasion: Scenic drive through boob-shaped mountains.

Amount: $2 USD.

Notes: No matter how many maps I show him, I just can't get Winston to see how sexy nature can be.

INFRACTION 16

August 19, 2005

"I told her my name was 'Frank Bancroft.' That may sound hard to remember, but it's actually just the last names of my 2 favorite women named Anne."

■ ■ ■

Location: Breakfast table.

Occasion: Post-sex debriefing and presentation of my award-winning lecture "How to Avoid Brunch with the Girl in Your Room . . . What? Yes, She's in There Right Now. I Know. Shhhhh. Keep it Down."

Amount: $15 USD.

Notes: Other fake names to give women (try finding me on Friendster now, ladies!):

- Archer Geddes*
- Taylor Green-Gables*
- Moises Purdue
- Belkis McFall
- Chester Slomba
- Fireworks Wilson
- Woodrow Gawiwi
- Lester Floriano
- Ike Beavers
- Hollis Tate
- Hydroplane Bactria
- Karl LaFong
- Tenzin Wangchuk
- Ernie Raisins
- Japheth Witmer
- Belvedere St. Croix
- Weldon Lundy
- Grover Roark
- Six Kicking Elk
- Devandra!
- Flip DesMangoes
- Nestor Cortez
- Q. R. Barnaby
- Josh Malmuth
- Berkley Johnson
- Rigiberto Sanchez
- Branches O'Toole

{ *denotes Anne-themed. }

INFRACTION 17

August 31, 2005

"If I were a black Scientologist, I would call myself L'Ron Hubbard."

■ ■ ■

Location: Bedroom.

Occasion: None.

Amount: $5 USD.

September 12, 2005

INFRACTION
18

"There is no finer piece of presex music than 'Rock You Like a Hurricane.' "

■ ■ ■

Location: Hallway.

Occasion: Frantic search for mix CD.

Amount: $5 USD.

Notes:

INFRACTION 19

September 19, 2005

“What kind of tanning salon doesn’t take Discover?”

■ ■ ■

Location: Horizons Tan & Spa.

Occasion: Twelve-minute base-coat touch-up.

Amount: $15 USD.

Notes: It pays to Discover. Or so I thought.

"I like piña coladas <u>OR</u> getting caught in the rain. But never both at the same time."

■ ■ ■

Location: Bar.

Occasion: Chance encounter with Rupert Holmes.

Amount: $18 USD.

Notes: Hey man, if you don't like strangers talking to you, stop writing genre-defining anthems.

October 5, 2005

"Pinot Grigio with lamb? Why not? Then I'll finish the night by anally inserting a beehive."

■ ■ ■

Location: Restaurant.

Occasion: First date.

Amount: $13 USD.

Notes: Also last date.

"What blind, thumbless child julienned this radish?"

■ ■ ■

Location: Park.

Occasion: Company picnic.

Amount: $15 USD.

Notes: Colleague who brought this was, in fact, blind. But still—Beethoven was deaf and you never saw him ruining picnics.

INFRACTION 23 *November 2, 2005*

■ ■ ■

Amount: $24 USD.

Notes: <u>SO</u> glad I went into that men's room.

"Just because I 'won' my People's Choice Award on eBay doesn't mean I didn't really win it."

■ ■ ■

Location: Bookshelf.

Occasion: Home tour.

Amount: $11 USD.

Notes: If you must know, I won "Favorite Daytime Serial."

INFRACTION 25

December 3, 2005

"Someone needs to tell Kathy Ireland that her ceiling fans are a joke."

■ ■ ■

Location: Griffith Park.

Occasion: Hiking with Nick, post 15-minute contemplative silence.

Amount: $22 USD.

Notes:

FROM THE DESK OF

SCHMIDT

Dear Miss Ireland:

As a future homeowner and admirer of fine ceiling fans, I feel it is my duty to convey to you a painful truth: you are the laughingstock of the overhead cooling industry. I'd be better off giving a friend two pieces of cardboard and telling him to spin.(Burn Notice, K.I. Thas' a how it's done, son.)

I realize that this might be hard to hear, but not nearly as hard as it is for people to hear one another over the incessant ambient buzzing of your terribly designed appliances.

At this point, no one would fault you for simply packing up your wares and leaving fanning to the professionals. However, if you wish to continue peddling ceiling fans, I've included some steps that, if implemented, *might* save your foundering enterprise.

FROM THE DESK OF

SCHMIDT

1) Stop "antiquing" everything. Who are you, Father Time? On the list of materials you use for your fans, draw a line through "treated copper" with a permanent marker.

2) Buffeting kills. An afternoon spent under a fan should not feel like an afternoon spent in a Mixed Martial Arts octagon. Smooth out your air displacement irregularities, pronto.

3) Find out who designs for Hampton Bay and *poach* them. Bad artists imitate. Great artists steal.

4) Align yourself with premium retailers. I'd buy flotsam from an airplane crash if they sold it at Design Within Reach. Just glue it to an Eames chair and name your price.

5) Be yourself.

This list is hardly exhaustive but should get you headed in the right direction. If you have any questions or concerns, please don't hesitate to contact me.

Sincerely,

Schmidt

P.S. I'd like to clarify that my disappointment in your line of ceiling fans has no bearing on my warm regard for your modeling career, which in my humble opinion was (and is) spectacular—both from an artistic and utilitarian (masturbatory) standpoint.

INFRACTION 26

December 14, 2005

"*MY* coffeehouse is a GNC."

■ ■ ■

Location: Starbucks bathroom line.

Occasion: Winston's little girl-sized bladder.

Amount: $15 USD.

Notes: If you rearrange the letters in "TALL," "GRANDE," "VENTI," "MOCHA," and "MOCHA-LITE" you get "I'M EAGER TO CHA-CHA TO APE LAND, LVNMFRP!"

"I wish I could cut off your other leg and put it over your mouth."

■ ■ ■

Location: Bus ride in Los Angeles.

Occasion: Nick's terrible idea.

Amount: $34 USD.

Notes: Nothing kills my public transportation buzz like a chatty amputee. But man, can they punch hard! Turns out strength is more important than balance.

2006

The Architecture of Love & Danger

■ ■ ■

TOTAL INFRACTIONS: 46

TOTAL AMOUNT: $756

INFRACTION 28 *January 6, 2006*

"I'd give her personality a 10, and her appearance a 2— making for an overall score of 2."

■ ■ ■

Location: Breakfast table.

Occasion: Blind date recap.

Amount: $9 USD.

Notes:

		Personality	Appearance	Overall Score
me	When being so harsh as to reduce fellow human beings to mere numbers, it is important to make sure I can withstand said microscope myself. If I can withstand, I may proceed in good conscience. If I can't, I must cease and desist. Here goes:	9	9	10
winston	Friends matter. To how *you* look. That's why Winston is like a great pair of penny loafers: adds shine, class, never distracts from the star:	5	7	7
nick	Nick is an interesting case. When I first met Nick I mistook him for a grumpy raisin. Now, through the confounding power of love and friendship, I look at him and see the beautiful, fresh green grape he carries inside. I'm not saying I'm happy about this development:	0	0	5

"How dare she parlay my desire to have sex with her tonight into a lunch date for tomorrow."

■ ■ ■

Location: Bar.

Occasion: Closing time.

Amount: $10 USD.

INFRACTION 30

January 11, 2006

"But strictly from an etymological point of view, shouldn't 'genocide' mean 'the systematic elimination of everyone named Geno?' "

■ ■ ■

Location: Holocaust Museum.

Occasion: Parents in town.

Amount: $2 USD.

Notes: Don't send me to college and expect me not to learn.

PATENT APPLICATION TRANSMITTAL

Patent Name: Rollerblade Shoehorn	Attorney Docket No.	0000000000000000000000001
	First Named Inventor	Schmidt
	Patent Issue Date (Month/Day/Year)	January 29, 2006

APPLICATION FOR: (Check applicable box) ☐ Utility Patent ☑ Design Patent ☐ Plant Patent

APPLICATION ELEMENTS

1. ☑ Fee Transmittal Form (Submit a duplicate copy)
2. ☑ Applicant claims small entity status.
3. ☑ Specification and Claims in double column copy of patent format (amended, if appropriate)
4. ☑ Drawing(s) (proposed amendments, if appropriate)
5. ☑ Reissue Oath/Declaration (original or copy)
6. ☐ Power of Attorney
7. ☐ Original U.S. Patent currently assigned? ☐ Yes ☑ No (If Yes, check applicable box(es))
   ☐ Written Consent of all Assignees
8. ☑ CD-ROM or CD-R in duplicate, Computer Program (Appendix) or large table
   ☐ Landscape Table on CD
9. Nucleotide and/or Amino Acid Sequence Submission (if applicable, items a. – c. are required))
   a. ☑ Computer Readable Form (CRF)
   b. Specification Sequence Listing on:
      i ☐ CD-ROM (2 copies) or CD-R (2 copies); or
      ii ☑ paper
   c. ☑ Statements verifying identity of above copies

ACCOMPANYING APPLICATION PARTS

10. ☑ Statement of status and support for all changes to the claims.
11. ☑ Foreign Priority Claim (if applicable)
12. ☑ Information Disclosure Statement (IDS)
    ☑ Copies of foreign patent documents, publications & other information
13. ☑ English Translation of Reissue Oath/Declaration (if applicable)
14. ☑ Preliminary Amendment
15. ☑ Return Receipt Postcard (MPEP 503) (Should be specifically itemized)
16. ☐ Other:

PATENT APPLICATION TRANSMITTAL

Patent Name: "The Isiah Thomas Guide to Thomas Guides"	Attorney Docket No.	000000000000000000000000
	First Named Inventor	Schmidt
	Patent Issue Date (Month/Day/Year)	January 29, 200

APPLICATION FOR: (Check applicable box) ☐ Utility Patent ☑ Design Patent ☐ Plant

APPLICATION ELEMENTS

1. ☑ Fee Transmittal Form (Submit a duplicate copy)
2. ☑ Applicant claims small entity status.
3. ☑ Specification and Claims in double column copy of patent format (amended, if appropriate)
4. ☑ Drawing(s) (proposed amendments, if appropriate)
5. ☑ Reissue Oath/Declaration (original or copy)
6. ☐ Power of Attorney
7. ☐ Original U.S. Patent currently assigned? ☐ Yes ☑ No (If Yes, check applicable box(es))
   ☐ Written Consent of all Assignees
8. ☑ CD-ROM or CD-R in duplicate, Computer Program (Appendix) or large table
   ☐ Landscape Table on CD
9. Nucleotide and/or Amino Acid Sequence Submission (if applicable, items a. – c. are required))
   a. ☑ Computer Readable Form (CRF)
   b. Specification Sequence Listing on:
      i ☐ CD-ROM (2 copies) or CD-R (2 copies); or
      ii ☑ paper
   c. ☑ Statements verifying identity of above copies

ACCOMPANYING APPLICAT

10. ☑ Statement of status and supp changes to the claims.
11. ☑ Foreign Priority Claim (if applicable)
12. ☑ Information Disclosure Sta
    ☑ Copies of foreign patent publications & other in
13. ☑ English Translation of (if applicable)
14. ☑ Preliminary Amendm
15. ☑ Return Receipt Pos (Should be specifi
16. ☐ Other:

■ ■ ■

Amount: $8 USD + $11 USD = $19 USD.

Notes: Patents Pending(s!):

INFRACTION 32

February 12, 2006

"I come for the Alpine, but I stay for the Nordic Combined."

■ ■ ■

Location: Couch.

Occasion: 2006 Winter Olympics, live from Turin!

Amount: $11 USD.

Notes: Five million years from now, people will have skis instead of feet.

"If you need proof that human beings are afraid to be happy, just look at the way polygamists dress their wives."

■ ■ ■

Location: Couch.

Occasion: *Big Love* series premiere.

Amount: $4 USD.

Notes: I'm sorry, but bonnets make me physically nauseous.

INFRACTION 34

March 28, 2006

"If anything, I think Coldplay is getting better."

■ ■ ■

Location: Hipster party.

Occasion: Nick's idea of a good time.

Amount: $16 USD.

Notes:

FROM THE DESK OF

SCHMIDT

Dear Gwyneth and Chris,

I was delighted to hear that you're pregnant again—and that Apple will have a little brother any day now. I don't know if this talented little fellow has a name yet, but if not, here are just a few ideas off the top of my head:

FROM THE DESK OF

SCHMIDT

Cork. Pudding. Sock. Bow. Toaster. Winch.
Gravel. Cranberries. Paper. Frame. Jar. Scissors.
Battery. Tape. Cup. Binder. Staple. Bananas.
Towel. Grass. Wheel. Basket. Log. Mustard.
Finger. Cuff. Broom. Cabinet. Key. Watch. Poi.
Oboe. Button. Photo. Tile. Book. Pumpkin. Pear.
Stick. Box. Velcro. Kettle. Plug. Hem. Pen. Dish.
Spoon. Collar. Spoke. Gun. Bench. Pole. Foot.
Tub. Bowl. Fork. Net. Pad. Hat. Saucer. Ball.
Sheet. Rind. Wall. Cream. Soap. Fig. Drapes.
Knuckle. Pin. Coal. Brush. Can. Bread. Phone.
Peel. Comb. Lid. Cord. Desk. Candle. Puddle.
Fax. Clock. Bullet. Pot. Fuse. Hinge. Balloon.
Cone. Latch. Canister. Mug. Splinter. Crumb.
Folder. Lamp. Cap. Glue. Cartridge. Pan. Purse.
Shoe. Glove. Handle. Mesh. Salsa. Bulb. Bracelet.
Pipe. Bag. Cigar. Suit. Pencil. Throat. Sink.
Gum. Knife. Case. Rug. Seed. Filter. Wood. Spork.
Pool. Bush. Corn. Sauce. Drain. Vat. Ridge.
Truck. Hole. Plate. Ink. Stamp. Cushion. Rock.
Sled. Dial. Suds. Coin. Strap. Chair. Wrench.
Rope. Zipper. Drawer. Dent. Floss. Oreo. Wallet.
Pie.

Sincerely,

Schmidt

P.S. Glass. Grout. Van. Fire. Clasp. Hair. Fence.
Valve. Hose. Goo. Nut.

April 7, 2006

"In the space program of my love life, we are currently at 'T-Minus Refractory Period.' "

■ ■ ■

Location: Kitchen.

Occasion: Sex break.

Amount: $34 USD.

Notes:

Photo Courtesy of Nick Miller

"She's my roast corn at a street fair. 364 days a year I forget she exists, but when the Fourth of July comes, no price is too steep."

■ ■ ■

Location: Front door.

Occasion: Nick asks "You're going to have sex with that cross-eyed Jet Blue flight attendant again?"

Amount: $16 USD.

Notes: Denise has a four-hour layover. Or should I say *LAID*-over???

April 20, 2006

"Sorry, but I just wouldn't feel comfortable dating a woman whose MySpace profile ***DOESN'T*** include a bikini pic."

■ ■ ■

Location: Tony Roma's for ribs.

Occasion: Dinner with Nick's family.

Amount: $25 USD.

Notes: Dear Mrs. Miller, Ask a forthright question and you're going to get a forthright answer. Sincerely, The Best Thing That Ever Happened to Your Son.

"You can't see it right now, but the lining on this jacket has quotes from *Pulp Fiction* printed on it."

■ ■ ■

Location: Dinner party.

Occasion: Dessert.

Amount: $11 USD.

Notes: The only thing better than having a secret is wearing one.

April 30, 2006

"Victoria's Secret can hang sexy pictures on the wall. *OR* they can sell aromatic lotion. But to do both is entrapment."

■ ■ ■

Location: Mall.

Occasion: Untimely erection.

Amount: $20 USD.

Notes: Heretofore unproduced scented lotions I think my penis would really cotton to:

- Erotic Wasabi
- Sage Un-Caged
- Rosemary Clooney
- Sinnamon
- Livin' in Plumerica
- Lemon Party: Lyme Thyme
- Strawberry Shortcake for Men
- Smokey Robinson
- Bath Salts, Shower Peppers
- Cucumber Unencumbered
- Aloe Vera Wang
- Honeysuckle
- Shea Margarine
- Bo Lavenderek
- Salty Denim
- Mangosteen Cilantro
- WD-69
- Naughty Biscotti
- Arabian? Nice!
- Jasmine-At-Work
- 80s Conversion Van-illa
- Zeus Juice
- Anything Not Made by a Weird Lip-Ringed Dude at Lush
- Frankincense Langella
- Old Spicy
- BBQ Jergen's
- Poinsettia Temptation
- Wanton Pecan
- Petal to the Metal
- Drakkar Noir He Didn't!
- Dr. Gus Abernathy's Wonder-Salve for Masturbation & The Treatment of Chicken Pox
- New Car

INFRACTION 40

May 16, 2006

GILL'S QUALITY 5-STAR DRY CLEANING

★★★★★

NAME Schmidt

PHONE/ADDRESS FILE | CHGE | ROUTE | TOTAL → | DATE

M T W TH F S

						AMOUNT	
SUITS			L		M		
SLACKS			L		M		
COATS			L		M		
SHIRTS			L		M		
SWEATERS			L		M		
DRESSES							
SKIRTS							
BLOUSES							

SPECIAL

128 Pairs of socks
9 scarves (wool)
9 scarves (silk)
3 Oven-Mits
1 Cape (Non-Reversible)
with "Purchase of Insurance."

■ ■ ■

Amount: $6 USD.

“If these walls could talk, they’d say ‘What color-blind dildo painted us ecru?’ ”

■ ■ ■

Location: New restaurant.

Occasion: Friends-only soft opening.

Amount: $29 USD.

Notes: If you don’t want the truth, don’t give me a comment card.

INFRACTION 42 *July 5, 2006*

Photo Courtesy of Nick Miller

■ ■ ■

Amount: $35 USD.

Notes: Streep + Tucci = perfect weekend.

"Let's be honest: When you said, 'Click to play video,' all I heard was, 'Click to masturbate.' "

■ ■ ■

Location: Apple store, Genius Bar.

Occasion: Calling out to Hot Genius as she's walking away.

Amount: $25 USD.

Notes: Who needs porn? I could masturbate all day to Apple's sleek modern designs.

July 23, 2006

"I'm donating my kidneys to science . . . and my heart to fashion."

■ ■ ■

Location: DMV.

Occasion: License renewal.

Amount: $14 USD.

Notes: If you don't look good in your driver's license photo, get the hell off the road.

July 26, 2006

INFRACTION 45

"Every trendsetting party needs at least one gorgeous bald woman."

■ ■ ■

Location: Art gallery.

Occasion: Distressing absence of bald women.

Amount: $14 USD.

Notes: Signs that you're at an "It" party:

- White scarves.
- African wildlife.
- I'm there.

July 30, 2006

"I can deal with camel toe, but not camel foot."

■ ■ ■

Location: Minneapolis.

Occasion: A brief glance in any direction.

Amount: $39 USD.

August 7, 2006

INFRACTION 47

"If Fight Club has a third rule—let's assume it's 'no gum chewing.' "

■ ■ ■

Location: Dodger Stadium.

Occasion: 7th inning stretch.

Amount: $5 USD.

August 11, 2006

"If you're looking for flattering lighting, you can't beat a candlelight vigil."

■ ■ ■

Location: Bathroom.

Occasion: Date-spot Q & A with apparent virgins Nick and Winston.

Amount: $5 USD.

Notes: Also not bad: right next to a fetal heart monitor or just outside a burning building.

"You owe it to yourself—and to the restaurant—to send back any fruit salad that's over 30% melon."

■ ■ ■

Location: Restaurant.

Occasion: Alleged papaya shortage.

Amount: $16 USD.

Notes:

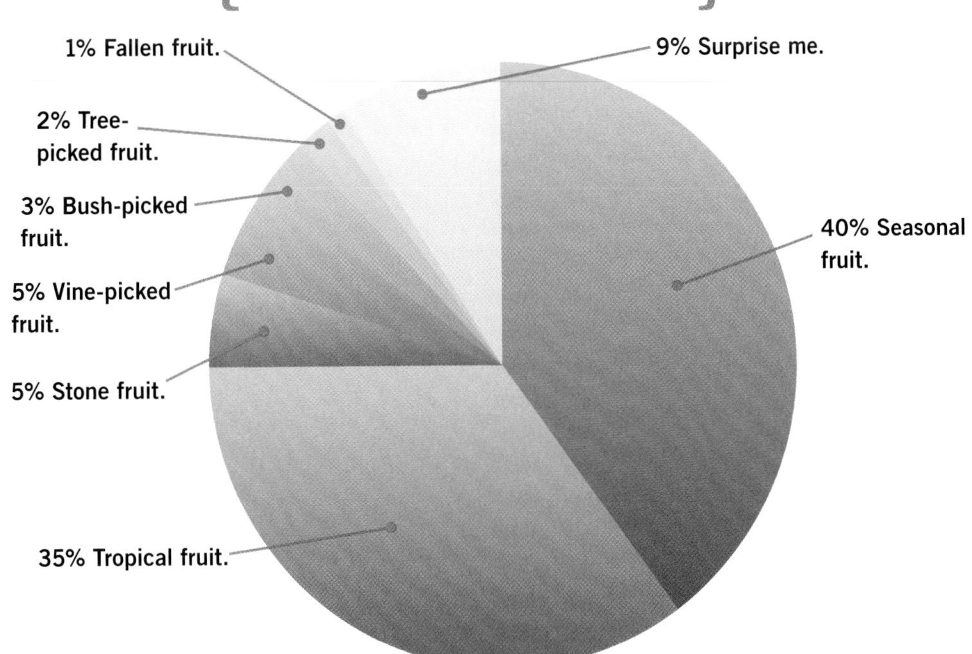

August 20, 2006

"If you're a crazy person who talks to himself—why not throw on a Bluetooth and at least LOOK productive?"

■ ■ ■

Location: Park.

Occasion: Croquet.

Amount: $14 USD.

Notes: Hold on a second, I'm confused, is it the "douchebag jar" or the "blue-ribbon-ideas jar?"

"Who is . . . Harriet Tubgirl!?"

■ ■ ■

Location: Couch.

Occasion: Answer to *Jeopardy* question: "Heroic custodian of the Underground Railroad."

Amount: $45 USD.

INFRACTION 52

August 30, 2006

"I'd sooner not make love than make love under fluorescent lights."

■ ■ ■

Location: Hospital.

Occasion: Donating blood.

Amount: $10 USD.

Notes: As God as my witness, here are the twenty-nine places I'll never make love again:

1. Nest of dryer sheets
2. Shipping container
3. Underfunded zoo
4. "Mom's Attic" section of U-Haul
5. Damp pleather
6. The 9th hole at Riviera Country Club
7. Aunt Bea's wake
8. Lazy River at Raging Waters
9. Dutch-made stepladder
10. Sensory-deprivation chamber
11. The fleeting cover of a solar eclipse
12. Non-claw-footed bathtub
13. Wasp country
14. Crate of packing peanuts
15. Scary forest at magic hour.
16. Tract housing development
17. Pile of bagels
18. Linoleum
19. Jennifer Convertibles showroom
20. Planetarium chair
21. Customs
22. "Abandoned" helipad
23. Porch swing
24. The post-sex wet spot
25. Racecar bed
26. Decommissioned naval destroyer
27. Under the boardwalk
28. Under fluorescent lights
29. Sacramento

INFRACTION 53

September 4, 2006

"The question is: Why don't ***YOU*** wear driving gloves?"

■ ■ ■

Location: Car.

Occasion: Late-night grocery run.

Amount: $5 USD.

Notes: If I had Nick's clammy tarantula hands, I'd wear gloves all the live-long day.

"I get all my best investment ideas during spin class."

■ ■ ■

Location: Computer.

Occasion: Mind-blowing day trade.

Amount: $14 USD.

Notes: I think it has something to do with compression shorts.

INFRACTION 55

September 12, 2006

"I have a date at nine. How long would it take to learn to play Incubus's 'Drive' on guitar?"

■ ■ ■

Location: Guitar Center.

Occasion: 7:45 PM.

Amount: $16 USD.

Notes: There is no denying the correlation between speed-of-finger movement and female arousal.

MUSICAL INSTRUMENT	RESULTING VAGINAL MOISTNESS (as measured by inverse coefficient of friction)
Saxophone (Alto, Tenor)	.68, .27
Tenor sax playing anything from *Miss Saigon*	.82
Bagpipe	.37
Bassoon	.19
Cymbals	.15
Flamenco guitar	1.00 (It's almost too much)
Appalachian dulcimer	.98
Guitar	.73
Harmonica	.17
Piano	.59
Recorder	.4
Triangle	.5
Tuba	.23
Vuvuzela	-.02
Flute	.61
Marimba	.05
Harp	.84
Jew's Harp	.92
Piccolo	.65
Bongo	.4
Kazoo	.0
Spoons	.15
Sleigh Bells	.2
Theramin	.89
Upright bass	.71

INFRACTION 56

September 21, 2006

Photo Courtesy of Nick Miller

■ ■ ■

Amount: $8 USD.

September 24, 2006

INFRACTION 57

"Does this visor look better forwards or backwards?"

■ ■ ■

Location: Front door.

Occasion: Frisbee Golf.

Amount: $14 USD.

Notes: I feel like "sideways" was also an option, but it's best to keep questions to Winston simple and direct.

INFRACTION 58 *September 28, 2006*

Photo Courtesy of Nick Miller

■ ■ ■

Amount: $12 USD.

September 29, 2006

INFRACTION 59

"This chair's not fit to be a lion-tamer's shield."

■ ■ ■

Location: Ikea main showroom.

Occasion: Furniture shopping.

Amount: $28 USD.

Notes: Nice try, Ilörk. Who do you think you are, Bengt?

INFRACTION 60

October 1, 2006

■ ■ ■

Amount: $22 USD.

Notes: If you want your boardwalk caricature to depict you in a kimono riding a giant origami crane, then I highly suggest wearing your kimono and bringing your crane.

"I'm about to take some sex and upgrade it from 'casual' to 'business casual.' "

■ ■ ■

Location: Bathroom.

Occasion: Emergency condom scrounge.

Amount: $7 USD.

Notes: "Black tie" is good too, but "white tie" is a game changer.

INFRACTION 62

October 6, 2006

Photo Courtesy of Nick Miller

■ ■ ■

Amount: $15 USD.

"I felt like some kind of frontier gynecologist: Drunk, authoritative, and elbows deep in Mae West."

■ ■ ■

Location: Breakfast table.

Occasion: Really weird dream.

Amount: $43 USD.

Notes: I remember exactly one snippet of dialogue from this dream and it's as follows:

ME: I need to speak with you about these meatballs.

MEDICINE MAN: Get out of my wigwam.

ME: I wish it were that easy.

October 10, 2006

"How come no Asian guys get tattoos of letters from ***OUR*** alphabet?"

■ ■ ■

Location: Batting cage.

Occasion: Strike two.

Amount: $7 USD.

Notes: Most people assume that if I could change one thing about Nick it would be the flatulence, but actually I'd love to make him Vietnamese.

"Sadly, the high sugar content of my semen precludes me from dating diabetic women."

■ ■ ■

Location: Wedding.

Occasion: Real big bridesmaid.

Amount: $33 USD.

Notes: Doctor's orders. Apparently it's like hummingbird food.

INFRACTION 66

October 19, 2006

"Someone needs to invent a teeth whitening system that's safe to use more than three times a day."

■ ■ ■

Location: Bathroom.

Occasion: Bleach tray comes out, whitestrip goes on.

Amount: $14 USD.

Notes:

{ IF I COULD WHITEN IT, WOULD I? }

BODY PART	YES, I'D WHITEN IT.	NO, I WOULDN'T WHITEN IT.	DEPENDS.
Nail beds	X		
Knuckle hair	X		
Palms	X		
White part of eyes	X		
Scalp	X		
Tongue	X		
Deep scrotum	X		
Extra elbow skin	X		
Butthole			X

October 23, 2006

INFRACTION 67

"It must be easy to rob a 911 dispatcher—'cause who are they gonna call?"

■ ■ ■

Location: Bedroom.

Occasion: Middle of night.

Amount: $13 USD.

Notes: The phrase "it's the perfect crime" gets bandied around a lot—but I think here it may actually apply.

INFRACTION 68

November 6, 2006

"Both girls have to be approximately the same size—otherwise it's like a threesome with Ren & Stimpy."

■ ■ ■

Location: Nightclub.

Occasion: Developing situation.

Amount: $19 USD.

Notes: Though if that's the way the cookie ends up crumbling, you're gonna want to start with Ren.

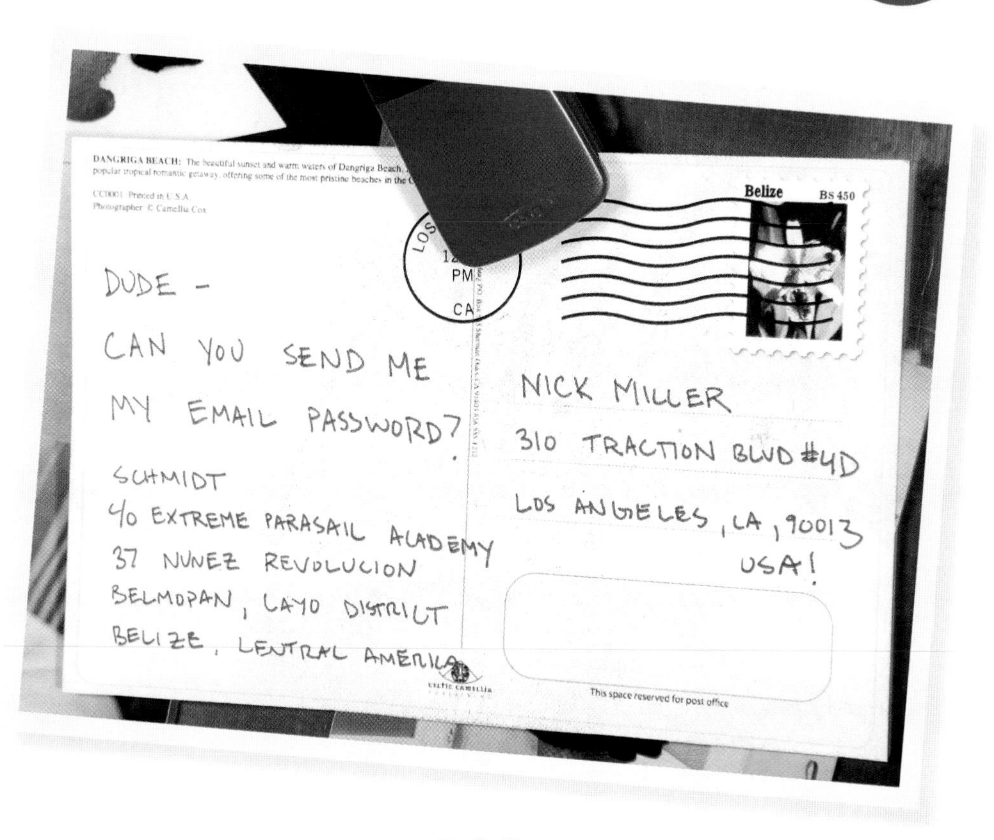

Photo Courtesy of Nick Miller

■ ■ ■

Amount: $14 USD.

Notes: Needless to say, Nick didn't send my password. Luckily, I remembered it was "cashmere18."

INFRACTION 70

November 28, 2006

"If I was a saucy billionaire, I would remake every single Charles Bronson movie with Bronson Pinchot."

■ ■ ■

Location: Couch.

Occasion: Serendipitous *Perfect Strangers* to *Deathwish* channel hop.

Amount: $3 USD.

Notes: Ironically, I have zero interest in seeing Charles Bronson play Balki Bartokomous. Go figure.

"This crossword puzzle is easier than getting laid at a bachelorette party at Curves! Ha-ha."

■ ■ ■

Location: Park bench.

Occasion: Lazy Sunday morning.

Amount: $13 USD.

INFRACTION 72

December 20, 2006

"The hair-care industry needs to ask itself one simple question: What will be our generation's 'Lather, rinse, repeat'?"

■ ■ ■

Location: Grocery store.

Occasion: Aisle 3.

Amount: $10 USD.

Notes:

How You Shampoo:	How I Shampoo:	How I Would Shampoo If All Time Constraints Were To Magically Fall Away:
Lather, rinse, repeat.	Lather, rinse. Lather, rinse. Lather, rinse, rinse, rinse. Repeat.	Lather, rinse. Lather, rinse. Lather, rinse, rinse, rinse. Towel dry, preliminary finger-style, blow-dry (no diffuser). Lather, rinse. Towel dry, secondary finger-style, blow-dry (with diffuser). Lather, rinse. Towel dry, final finger-style, air dry hanging upside down on monkey bars. Repeat.

"Football? I just assumed a movie called *We Are Marshall* was about a schizophrenic guy named Marshall."

■ ■ ■

Location: Movie theater.

Occasion: Closing credits of *We Are Marshall* (whispered through light tears).

Amount: $12 USD.

Notes: Though the trailer makes a lot more sense now.

2007

Freedom/Pain

■ ■ ■

TOTAL INFRACTIONS: 28

TOTAL AMOUNT: $437

February 8, 2007

"Who would've guessed that TrimSpa would be the only medication that ***DIDN'T*** kill Anna Nicole Smith?"

■ ■ ■

Location: Couch.

Occasion: Death of Anna Nicole Smith.

Amount: $10 USD.

Notes: Are you kidding? This should have been TrimSpa's new slogan.

"In the oatmeal game, it's steel-cut or ***BE*** cut."

■ ■ ■

Location: Denny's.

Occasion: Breakfast.

Amount: $16 USD.

March 10, 2007

"Sting was in a band?"

■ ■ ■

Location: Bar.

Occasion: "Roxanne" on jukebox.

Amount: $40 USD.

April 2, 2007

INFRACTION 77

"This menu is outrageous. Okra is no more a root vegetable than it is a tennis racket. And when are you going to stop shoving ramps down my throat?"

■ ■ ■

Location: Gastropub.

Occasion: Conversation with local chef.

Amount: $19 USD.

April 10, 2007

"You'll know it's summer because I'll be wearing a tank top."

■ ■ ■

Location: Target.

Occasion: The making of a promise.

Amount: $8 USD.

Notes: And you'll know it's fall because everyone will be saying, "Schmidt, we miss your tank top."

"Gentlemen, welcome to the closed-toe-shoe Event Horizon."

■ ■ ■

Location: Bloomingdale's.

Occasion: 2007 Friends & Family Sale.

Amount: $5 USD.

May 24, 2007

"If I had a penny for every time someone mispronounces 'bruschetta' in my presence I'd be a billionaire."

■ ■ ■

Location: Wine bar.

Occasion: Ignorant waiter #10006-B.

Amount: $14 USD.

Notes: For the last time: It's a soft "ch,," almost an "shh," but not quite. So for the love of God just take a second, think about what you're doing, then split the difference between "lunch" and "hush," you animal.

June 11, 2007

INFRACTION 81

"It's squash blossoms or it's nothing!"

■ ■ ■

Location: Farmer's market.

Occasion: Squash blossom season.

Amount: $14 USD.

Notes: Squash blossom season is short and fickle, and should never be wasted.

June 18, 2007

"If you still have a tile countertop, you better be living in Central America."

■ ■ ■

Location: Home Depot.

Occasion: Mop shopping.

Amount: $19 USD.

Notes: Porous grout? On a cooking surface? Let's just cut out the middleman and eat off a turd.

"If I had your face shape, I'd wear a loose-weave knit cap every single day of the year."

■ ■ ■

Location: Beach.

Occasion: Conversation with 4th grader.

Amount: $12 USD.

June 29, 2007

"Everyone, I have an announcement to make: My new style icon animal is the killer whale."

■ ■ ■

Location: Dinner table.

Occasion: Dinner.

Amount: $10 USD.

Notes: Black. White. Simple. Done.

"I mean, come on, I shouldn't have to drive to Alhambra to find artisanal gherkins."

■ ■ ■

Location: Dinner table.

Occasion: Gherkinless meal.

Amount: $11 USD.

July 14, 2007

"Putting a full-tang handle on a cheese knife is like mounting a bazooka on a Razor scooter."

■ ■ ■

Location: Sur la Table.

Occasion: Pushy saleslady.

Amount: $7 USD.

"I consider myself the Che Guevara of the lychee martini revolution."

■ ■ ■

Location: The Umlaut Lounge.

Occasion: *EXCELLENT* lych-tini.

Amount: $29 USD.

August 11, 2007

"If Diplo was a stock, I would buy, buy, buy."

■ ■ ■

Location: Concert.

Occasion: An American artist on the ones and twos.

Amount: $22 USD.

"Sometimes all it takes is an apostrophe to turn 'manslaughter' into 'man's laughter.' "

■ ■ ■

Location: Wedding reception.

Occasion: Best man toast.

Amount: $30 USD.

Notes: In retrospect, I may have boxed myself in by titling the toast "Man's Laughter" before I'd written it.

INFRACTION 90

September 7, 2007

Photo Courtesy of Nick Miller

■ ■ ■

Amount: $23 USD.

Amount: Dear Color Me Mine, If you would like to use this in your brochure, please feel free.

"Seeing Nick with his shirt off is like seeing a hermit crab between shells."

■ ■ ■

Location: Bathroom.

Occasion: Shell change.

Amount: $6 USD.

Notes: Sorry, crabs.

INFRACTION 92 — *September 19, 2007*

"Here's my recipe for snack mix at a bar: 3 parts nuts, 5,000 parts urine."

■ ■ ■

Location: Bar.

Occasion: Offering of snack mix.

Amount: $8 USD.

Notes: Afraid you're getting too much urine and not enough feces? Try the popcorn.

"I really need to get a tattoo on my calf. But which calf?"

■ ■ ■

Location: Kitchen.

Occasion: Lunch.

Amount: $16 USD.

Notes: I'm thinking left. Though some people say that's "the gay calf . . ." Possible solution: address the gay thing head on, get a tattoo of t.A.T.u. (one lesbian per calf) and rub calves together for hot inky make-out.

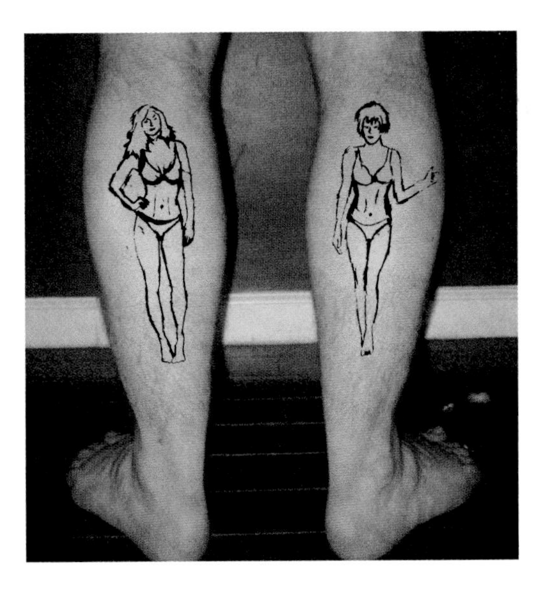

October 5, 2007

"Will tonight finally be the night where everybody Wang Chungs?"

■ ■ ■

Location: Car.

Occasion: Driving to Vegas.

Amount: $6 USD.

"If a pony only doing one trick has become synonymous with failure, perhaps we as a society have become too demanding of our ponies."

■ ■ ■

Location: Strip club.

Occasion: Unfair criticism of Kandy.

Amount: $18 USD.

November 1, 2007

"First rule of real estate: Never live more than three miles from your dojo."

■ ■ ■

Location: A friend's new pad.

Occasion: Lease signing.

Amount: $15 USD.

Notes: That's not just the first rule, that's the only rule.

November 16, 2007

INFRACTION **97**

"If these raspberries are organic, then I'm Mary Poppins."

■ ■ ■

Location: Co-op.

Occasion: Lying hippie.

Amount: $13 USD.

Notes: I didn't fall off the veggie-diesel turnip truck yesterday, *Isaac*.

November 27, 2007

Photo Courtesy of Nick Miller

Photo Courtesy of Nick Miller

■ ■ ■

Amount: $9 USD + $12 USD = $21 USD.

Notes: The Annual Turkey Trot 5K is about to take it in the face.

"Does everyone remember the rules of '8-on-8 Strip Dreidel'?"

■ ■ ■

Location: Dinner table.

Occasion: First night of Hanukkah.

Amount: $5 USD.

Notes: The eight people on each team represent the eight nights of Hanukkah. And the nipple clamps represent friendship.

INFRACTION 100

December 12, 2007

"God, I wish I had the wrists for a Livestrong bracelet."

■ ■ ■

Location: Mall.

Occasion: Escalator ride.

Amount: $20 USD.

Notes:

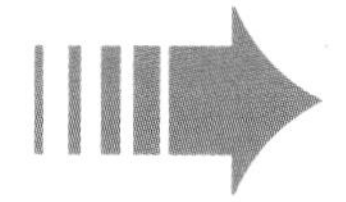

{ PERSONAL CHARITY NAMES STILL UP FOR GRABS: }

Name Of Charity	Benefitting
Schmidt's Mitts	Inner-city children with little or no access to quality, designer gloves.
Tomorrow's Crotch	Vasectomy survivors and their families.
March of Hundred Dollar Bills Y'all!	Whatever the hell March of Dimes does . . . but exactly 1,000 times better.
Borders Without Doctors	Chain bookstore employees lacking adequate health care.
Fallopia's List	Something related to breasts or the whatchamacallit.
House's House	Adults diagnosed with any disease ever mentioned on the television show *House, M.D.*
House's Clubhouse	Children diagnosed with any disease ever mentioned on the television show *House, M.D.*
The Salvation Army of Darkness	Bruce Campbell.
Friends of Enemies of the California Elephant Seal	Poachers who poach ugly things.
Red Cross, White Koran, Blue Menorah	TBD.
National 5-H Council	Child farmers of the future.
Three Cups of Schmidt	Tea, Afghanistan.
Cave-Savers	Victims of spelunking accidents.
Cave-Savers Africa	Victims of spelunking accidents & HIV.
Cave-Savers South Africa	Victims of spelunking accidents & HIV & unfair characterization in the Stephen Dorff vehicle *Power of One.*
God's Mistake	The left-handed.

INFRACTION 101

December 28, 2007

"Khloe is at her best when she's playing Niles to Kourtney's Frasier."

■ ■ ■

Location: Couch.

Occasion: *Keeping up with the Kardashians* season finale.

Amount: $20 USD.

2008

Innocence Found

■ ■ ■

TOTAL INFRACTIONS: 25

TOTAL AMOUNT: $444

January 1, 2008

"You ask: 'Ginger or Mary Ann?' But I ask: 'Who has the less chafey hammock?' "

■ ■ ■

Location: Couch.

Occasion: *Gilligan's Island* New Year's Day marathon.

Amount: $7 USD.

Notes: Answer: Mrs. Howell.

January 19, 2008

INFRACTION 103

"Just once before I die, I'd like to meet someone who has seen a dental dam."

■ ■ ■

Location: Crowded elevator.

Occasion: None.

Amount: $28 USD.

INFRACTION 104 *February 24, 2008*

"They should have called it: 'There Will Be Blood . . . There *WON'T* Be Titties.' "

■ ■ ■

Location: Oscar party.

Occasion: The 80th Annual Academy Awards.

Amount: $16 USD.

March 1, 2008

INFRACTION 105

"If you ask me, the packaging for condoms and moist towelettes is far too similar."

■ ■ ■

Location: Tony Roma's for Ribs.

Occasion: Dinner with Nick's family.

Amount: $31 USD.

Notes:

Q: Which is worse, thinking you have a condom in your wallet and it turns out to be a moist towelette—or the other way around?

A: Holy crap, that's a tough one. How sticky are my hands?

INFRACTION 106 *March 4, 2008*

"Just hypothetically: How hot would a girl have to be for you to overlook a swastika tramp stamp?"

■ ■ ■

Location: Kitchen.

Occasion: None.

Amount: $27 USD.

■ ■ ■

Amount: $3 USD.

Notes: Last time I buy a label maker with *THAT* font.

INFRACTION 108 *March 28, 2008*

"A female bartender who wears a wedding ring is like a soldier who sticks a cork in his gun!"

■ ■ ■

Location: Bar.

Occasion: Married bartender who apparently hates money.

Amount: $7 USD.

Notes: Other things an openly married bartender is like: 

- A fireman who crams an orange in his hose!
- A yachtsman who dips his sails in cement!
- A supermodel who puts on a beekeeper's mask!
- A whaler who lashes a pillow to his harpoon!
- A miner who installs curtains on his headlamp!
- A cowboy who covers his lasso with lube!
- A porn star who ties a knot in his dick!

April 1, 2008

"When it comes to back-pocket embroidery on denim, more is more."

■ ■ ■

Location: Hollywood Bowl.

Occasion: Urinal queue.

Amount: $29 USD.

Notes: But when it comes to darts on a dress shirt, more is never enough.

"I wish my head were like eight percent bigger in relation to my body. No wait, seven percent."

■ ■ ■

Location: Fun House mirror.

Occasion: Affordable opportunity to sample alternate head-sizes.

Amount: $2 USD.

Notes: Reality check: Anything more than a seven percent increase and I turn into an encephalitic Ralph Macchio.

May 5, 2008

" 'Yesterday' is the new 'tomorrow.' "

■ ■ ■

Location: Bed, Bath & Beyond.

Occasion: Linens re-up.

Amount: $24 USD.

Notes: Labeling "what" is the new "what" is a fluid process. "Something" that is the new "something" at this very minute—might no longer be the new something five minutes from now. As I write this, the following are 100 percent true. Five minutes from now? Don't quote me! ("Don't quote me!" is the new "Sock it to me!")

"Farm-raised salmon" is the new "Beef jerky."

"Kitchen supply stores" are the new "Discos."

"Skateboarders" are the new "Rapists."

"After-parties" are the new "Church."

"Black" is the new "Dark black."

"Drunk" is the new "Sober."

"Easter" is the new "Vernal Equinox."

"Marbles" are the new "Hopscotch."

"Pork" is the new "Bayer Aspirin."

"James Franco" is the new "Regis."

"Grass" is the new "Dirt."

"Carl" is the new "Greg."

"Lazy eyes" are the new "Huge tits."

May 20, 2008

"I'll know my pecs are the perfect size when there's three finger widths' clearance between my stomach and T-shirt."

■ ■ ■

Location: Gym.

Occasion: New personal trainer.

Amount: $11 USD.

Note: Three *ADULT* finger widths.

May 23, 2008

INFRACTION 113

"Pssst! Wake up. I just realized that people getting treated for cancer don't have to wax."

■ ■ ■

Location: Nick's bedroom.

Occasion: 4 AM.

Amount: $48 USD.

June 2, 2008

Amount: $16 USD.

Notes: Like a rock . . . except harder.

"Can you still see my delts when I'm wearing this poncho?"

■ ■ ■

Location: Front door.

Occasion: Rainy day.

Amount: $13 USD.

June 19, 2008

"Skinny Chandler makes me laugh, but puffy Chandler makes me think."

■ ■ ■

Location: Couch.

Occasion: Heated game of Scene It: *Friends* Edition.

Amount: $5 USD.

June 28, 2008

Photo Courtesy of Nick Miller

■ ■ ■

Amount: $21 USD.

Notes: The San Diego Zoo is awesome.

July 2, 2008

"Paramilitary groups get a bad rap—but I think it's brave that handicapped people want to serve."

■ ■ ■

Location: Couch.

Occasion: Successful rescue of fifteen hostages being held by FARC.

Amount: $25 USD.

July 3, 2008

INFRACTION 119

"I wish there were more places I could play indoor beach volleyball."

■ ■ ■

Location: Couch.

Occasion: Sweet Peter Horton line in *Side Out.*

Amount: $19 USD.

INFRACTION 120

August 8, 2008

"Pageantry has a new address . . . and it's spelled 'Beijing.' "

■ ■ ■

Location: Couch.

Occasion: 2008 Summer Olympics, opening ceremonies.

Amount: $8 USD.

Photo Courtesy of Nick Miller

■ ■ ■

Amount: $25 USD.

Notes: Someone needs to tell Alexander Graham Bell that Nick has his phone.

September 1, 2008

"If I were a tiger I would ***LINE UP*** to be shot by Vladimir Putin."

■ ■ ■

Location: Couch.

Occasion: Russia is back!

Amount: $13 USD.

Photo Courtesy of Nick Miller

■ ■ ■

Amount: $14 USD.

Notes: Do I build Lego sushi because it's beautiful, or because I secretly hope Nick will get stoned and eat it? I'm not even sure _I_ know.

November 4, 2008

“Barack got me in the booth, but Michelle made me pull the lever.”

■ ■ ■

Location: Community Center.

Occasion: 2008 Presidential Election.

Amount: $10 USD.

"Actually, mine DOESN'T stink. It's a very rare medical condition, thank you very much."

■ ■ ■

Location: Rowboat.

Occasion: Double date.

Amount: $29 USD.

Notes: Hey, she asked.

INFRACTION 126

December 1, 2008

"Nick, must all tarps be blue?"

■ ■ ■

Location: Roof.

Occasion: Leak.

Amount: $13 USD.

Notes: Where is it written that waterproof = dull?

2009

Musings, Fumblings, and Cheese

▪ ▪ ▪

TOTAL INFRACTIONS: 36
TOTAL AMOUNT: $549

January 1, 2009

"Only 185 days until breakfast at Wimbledon!"

■ ■ ■

Location: New Year's Eve party.

Occasion: 12:01 AM.

Amount: $20 USD.

January 11, 2009

INFRACTION 128

"Sideburns are for rockabillies and leprechauns."

■ ■ ■

Location: Mirage Salon & Wax.

Occasion: Nick's semi-annual haircut.

Amount: $9 USD.

Notes: As a nondeformed person, I have no reason to grow facial hair. But for those who choose to do so, I highly recommend the following facial hair concepts:

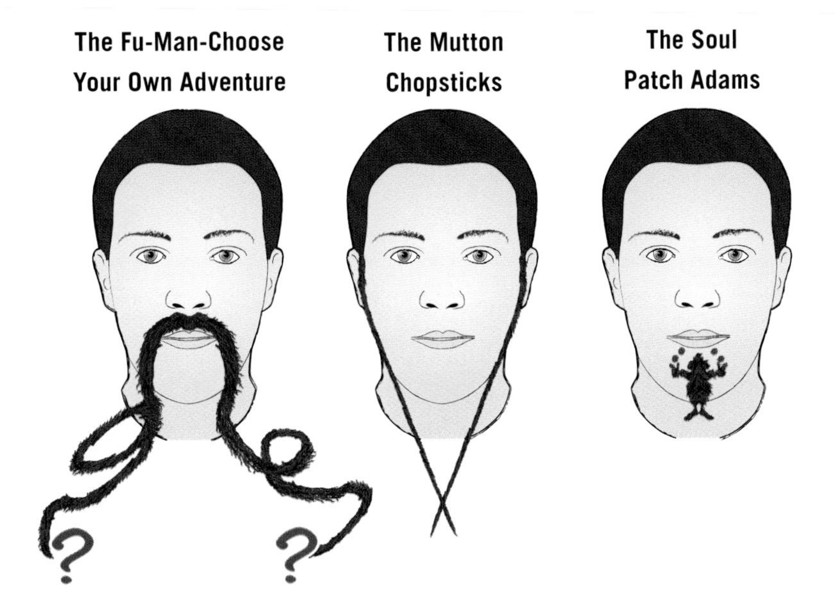

INFRACTION 129 *January 24, 2009*

"You laugh now, but my sons will be fighting over this selvage muslin tie at my funeral."

■ ■ ■

Location: Upscale men's boutique (location withheld).

Occasion: Legacy purchase.

Amount: $12 USD.

Notes: Finished: Buying clothes for now. Starting? Buying clothes for always.

“If I went to graduate school, it would be to study why people can be sexually attracted to cartoons.”

■ ■ ■

Location: Couch.

Occasion: First rewatching of *Who Framed Roger Rabbit* since childhood.

Amount: $1 USD.

Notes: There's just something about Weasel #2 that gets me half-erect . . .

"Don't just text her—
SUBtext her."

■ ■ ■

Location: Nick's room.

Occasion: Classic ham-fisted Nick Miller booty call.

Amount: $12 USD.

Notes: For example:

What You're Texting:
I Don't Play Games.

What You're Subtexting:
I Do Play Games.

What You're Texting:
N-E-1 4 69?

What You're Subtexting:
If You Can Read This You Need This.

What You're Texting:
Lol.

What You're Subtexting:
(Nothing. When You Text "Lol" You Are Texting Nothing, You Slack-Jawed Dipshit.)

INFRACTION 132

March 2, 2009

"The only thing that Don Johnson ever did wrong was stop making *Nash Bridges.*"

■ ■ ■

Location: Track.

Occasion: Jogging.

Amount: $12 USD.

Notes: If you only lose your virginity to one late-nineties detective show, make it *Bridges.**

*Ideally a Cheech-heavy episode like "Frisco Blues."

"Recognize this bowler hat? You will. It's about to win gold in the 50-yard haberdash."

■ ■ ■

Location: Cusp of fashion history.

Occasion: None.

Amount: $12 USD.

April 5, 2009

"I see myself as a missionary for the Church of Eminem."

■ ■ ■

Location: Sidewalk in front of Mormon Temple.

Occasion: Fascinating conversation with fellow missionaries.

Amount: $13 USD.

“No shape flatters the clavicle quite like a W.”

■ ■ ■

Location: Bar.

Occasion: Happy hour.

Amount: $20 USD.

Notes:

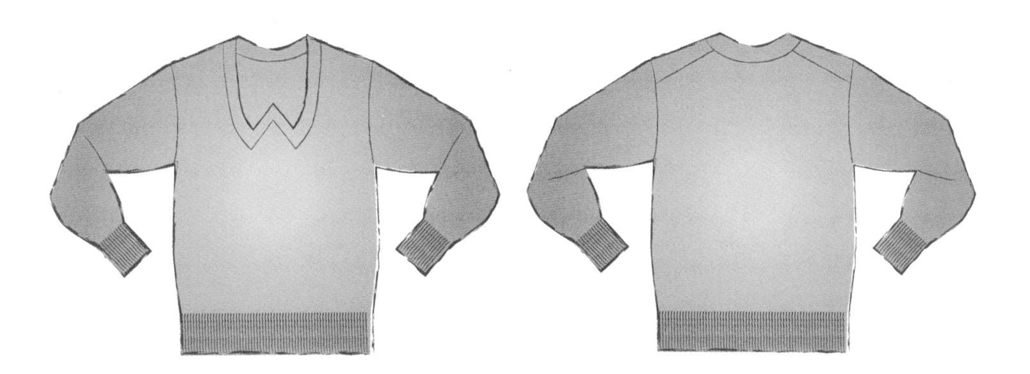

April 28, 2009

"If I'm cremated, I want my remains to play dandruff in a Head & Shoulders commercial."

■ ■ ■

Location: Lunch.

Occasion: None.

Amount: $16 USD.

"It's no accident there's a 'quest' in the middle of 'Equestrian.

■ ■ ■

Location: Couch.

Occasion: The 135th running of the Kentucky Derby.

Amount: $8 USD.

Notes: Horse names to consider:

- Nickels & Wonder
- Excalibur Jazz
- Shod by God
- Lightning Un-bottled
- Neverglue
- Italian Stallion II
- What's the Deal with Soft Drinks?
- Violent Ennui
- Hung Like a Schmidt
- Horse: Radish
- Horse d'Oeuvres
- Horsing Around the World in Eighty Days
- 9–11 Avenged
- Mike
- Rocket with a Saddle
- Arby's Presents: Sauce Comma Horsey
- The Dwarf Conveyance
- Kablammo!!!
- Flesh Bike
- Stirrups of Destiny
- Rippling Haunches
- Sunrise Equator
- Longface McNostrils
- Dame Hugh Laurie
- Alphabet Quandry
- Unbreakable Legs Knock Wood
- Realizing Deuteronomy
- Coltz II Men

INFRACTION 138

May 3, 2009

"I applaud the makers of women's jeans for what they've done vis-á-vis the side view. Now let's dig in on the rearview, boys."

■ ■ ■

Location: Outdoor café.

Occasion: Just some good old-fashioned butt-watching.

Amount: $15 USD.

"I present to you the finest Mexican pâté on the planet: 'Foie Gracias!' "

■ ■ ■

Location: Cinco de Mayo party.

Occasion: The Invention of Foie Gracias.

Amount: $5 USD.

Notes:

{RECIPE FOR "FOIE-GRACIAS":}

INGREDIENTS

1/2 lb. piece raw Grade A duck foie gras at room temperature, cleaned and deveined.

Salt and pepper to taste.

2 tsp canola oil.

2 tbsp balsamic vinegar.

SPECIAL EQUIPMENT

10-inch heavy skillet.

Piñata.

Sombrero (festive, not lazy).

Gypsy Kings CD.

PREPARATION

After deveining, cut the foie gras crosswise into 1/2-inch-thick pieces, then season with salt and pepper. Heat 1 teaspoon of the canola oil in a 10-inch heavy skillet over moderately high heat until hot but not smoking. Sauté half the foie gras until golden, 45 to 60 seconds on each side (it will be pink inside). Quickly transfer to a paper towel to drain and discard fat in skillet. Sauté the rest of the foie gras the same way, then discard all but 1 tablespoon of remaining fat in skillet. Add 2 tablespoons balsamic vinegar and bring to a boil. Serve foie gras with sauce, Fritos, and an enthusiastic "AYE-YIE-YIE-YIE!!!"

May 24, 2009

"If anyone runs into Salman Rushdie tonight, tell him I have a great idea for a syndicated column called 'Don't Rush Me.' "

■ ■ ■

Location: Event space.

Occasion: Michael Chabon's birthday party.

Amount: $27 USD.

"If we accept that A: she has not worked in forty years, yet B: can still afford Lakers floor seats . . . we must conclude C: Dyan Cannon is a financial genius."

■ ■ ■

Location: Couch.

Occasion: 2009 NBA Finals.

Amount: $6 USD.

June 11, 2009

"I feel like this shawl collar almost makes me look TOO regal."

▪ ▪ ▪

Location: Beach.

Occasion: Bonfire.

Amount: $16 USD.

Notes: Nobody wants to be the "regal bonfire guy."

"Have the girls of *Girls Gone Wild* actually *GONE* wild? Or was wild their natural state all along?"

■ ■ ■

Location: Couch.

Occasion: *Girls Gone Wild: Divas of Daytona*

Amount: $10 USD.

Notes: Talk about an unanswerable question. I might as well have asked "How much does God weigh?"

INFRACTION 144 *June 25, 2009*

"I never cared for Michael Jackson's music, but I sure did admire the way he lived."

■ ■ ■

Location: Centralized outpouring of sorrow.

Occasion: Death of Michael Jackson.

Amount: $12 USD.

Notes:

June 29, 2009

INFRACTION 145

"The Surf was delicious, but the Turf was amateur-hour."

■ ■ ■

Location: Stuart Anderson's Black Angus.

Occasion: Work function.

Amount: $15 USD.

Notes: This place is one stolen "G" away from being "Stuart Anderson's Black Anus."

INFRACTION 146

July 1, 2009

"So I was at ████ with ████ and we saw this ████ with sunglasses and we realized it was ████████. Anyway, I walked up to her and we started talking about ████. We ended up going to ████ and ███ around in the ████ and also a little bit in the ████ but not in the ████ because ████ showed up. Then, afterwards, I overheard Madonna make a really racist joke."

■ ■ ■

Location: Kitchen.

Occasion: Three-Day weekend.

Amount: $45 USD.

Notes: (Infraction redacted for legal reasons.)

"Get outta my dreams . . . and onto my Sea-Doo!"

■ ■ ■

Location: Lake Havasu.

Occasion: HavaBlast 2009!

Amount: $21 USD.

July 18, 2009

"My conception of Heaven is based entirely on the visual aesthetic of Cirque du Soleil."

■ ■ ■

Location: Couch.

Occasion: *Defending Your Life*, commercial break.

Amount: $5 USD.

"You haven't had intercourse until you've had intercourse in a gazebo."

■ ■ ■

Location: Los Angeles Superior Courthouse.

Occasion: Jury duty.

Amount: $29 USD.

Notes: Guilty as charged!

INFRACTION 150

September 2, 2009

"Los Angeles has the most qualified local newscasters in the world."

■ ■ ■

Location: Couch.

Occasion: Accu-Weather out-accurates Regular Weather once again.

Amount: $5 USD.

Photo Courtesy of Nick Miller

■ ■ ■

Amount: $4 USD.

October 14, 2009

"Final score? Plucking 1, Threading 0."

■ ■ ■

Location: Koreatown.

Occasion: Immense pain and redness.

Amount: $11 USD.

“When it comes to trannies, I say: Fool me once, shame on you. Fool me twice, shame on your excellent use of eye shadow.”

■ ■ ■

Location: West Hollywood.

Occasion: Halloween.

Amount: $33 USD.

November 3, 2009

"Even the widest tie dreams of one day being skinny."

■ ■ ■

Location: Thrift store.

Occasion: Costume shopping for "Ballerz v. Shot Callerz: Hip-Hop Supreme Court" party.

Amount: $18 USD.

Notes: 

{ THEME PARTY IDEAS FOR THE FUTURE: }

"Jet Packs n' Lingerie"

"Sexy Sandinistas: Deep in Naked-ragua"

"Chutes & Ladders & Causeways & Easements: Municipal Orgy 2010"

"Leaping Salmon, Gaping Bear Mouth."

"Stringer's Funeral:
Commemorating the expiration of all
'Spoiler Alert' Claims on *The Wire* and *One Tree-Hill*"

"Confident Squires, Insolent Maidens"

"Remake of *Kinsey* with Attractive People"

"Norse Jackee: Vikings + *227* + Edie Falco =???"

INFRACTION
155

November 10, 2009

"If the only thing that comes out of this whole swine flu nonsense is that surgical masks finally have their style moment, then I'm for it."

■ ■ ■

Location: LAX International terminal.

Occasion: Pocket of Asian people.

Amount: $18 USD.

"I would describe myself as fiscally Team Edward, and socially Team Jacob."

■ ■ ■

Location: Shower.

Occasion: None.

Amount: $5 USD.

Notes: Stop eavesdropping when I'm talking to myself in the shower, Nick.

INFRACTION 157

November 22, 2009

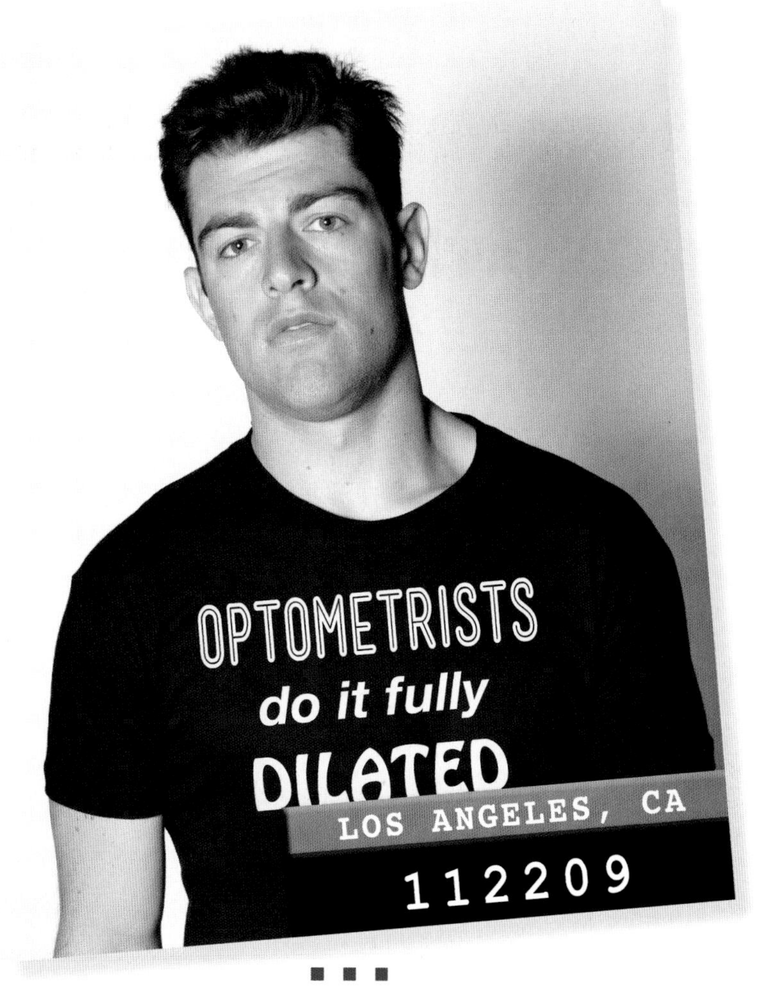

Photo Courtesy of Los Angeles Police Department

■ ■ ■

Location: Very small riot.

Occasion: LA Galaxy get screwed on PKs.

Amount: $9 USD.

Notes: Never wear flip-flops to jail.

"I had her revved up like an ice cream truck on the freeway."

■ ■ ■

Location: Bathroom.

Occasion: Shaving.

Amount: $11 USD.

Notes:

{ SONGS I'D LIKE TO HEAR AS AN ICE-CREAM TRUCK JINGLE: }

"Rumpshaker"

"Invisible Touch"

"2 Legit 2 Quit"

That one that goes "When you get caught between the moon and New York Ciiiiityyyyyyy . . ."

"Strokin' "

INFRACTION 159

December 23, 2009

"Here's how I define 'pashmina': A slightly wider scarf that 'society' says I'm not allowed to wear."

■ ■ ■

Location: Barney's Co-Op.

Occasion: Shortcut through women's section.

Amount: $11 USD.

December 29, 2009

INFRACTION 160

"WAZZZZZZZZZZZZUPPPPPPPPPPPPP???"

■ ■ ■

Location: Airport baggage claim.

Occasion: Nick returns from Chicago.

Amount: $40 USD.

Notes: How much longer are we going to wait to bring this back?

INFRACTION 161

December 30, 2009

"Remember, guys: Beer before sherry, everything's merry. Beer before spritzer, end up kissing Wolf Blitzer."

■ ■ ■

Location: Hooters.

Occasion: Dispensing of valuable advice.

Amount: $25 USD.

Notes: I just want everyone to be safe and have a good time.

December 31, 2009

INFRACTION
162

"If I could come up with a good DJ name, so many of my problems would be solved."

■ ■ ■

Location: Bathroom.

Occasion: None.

Amount: $18 USD.

Notes:

{ DJ NAMES SO FAR: }

FoxTown

Schmidtio

2010

Farewell Andromeda

■ ■ ■

TOTAL INFRACTIONS: 40
TOTAL AMOUNT: $631

INFRACTION 163 *January 9, 2010*

"Why would I buy the entire Godfather trilogy when I only like Part III?"

■ ■ ■

Location: Garage sale.

Occasion: Antiquing season is always right around the corner.

Amount: $7 USD.

Notes:

What The Coppola Brand Has:	What The Coppola Brand Needs:
Dynastic Hollywood Empire.	More Sofia the actress, less Sofia the director.
Vineyards.	A non-vomit-inducing Syrah.
Mystique.	Another collaboration with Bram Stoker.
	Limited-edition Vespa.
	Touring Magic Show "Apocalypse Wow!"
	Remake starring Gene Hackman as an aging professional wrestler named "The Conversation."
	To lay off the Italian thing for like a year.
	HGTV show *Tucker: The Man and His Dream . . . House.*
	Sex tape.

"If it's not Top 40 and I can't Dougie to it, I don't want it anywhere near my Zune."

■ ■ ■

Location: Club.

Occasion: Sorely misguided DJ.

Amount: $22 USD.

January 19, 2010

“If lovemaking is an international chain of stores, I am the flagship!”

■ ■ ■

Location: Bedroom.

Occasion: Moment of ejaculation.

Amount: $40 USD.

January 25, 2010

INFRACTION 166

"Is there a more loathed yet oddly tragic figure than the pre-Internet pedophile?"

■ ■ ■

Location: Dinner Table.

Occasion: Verdict in the Gary Glitter trial.

Amount: $15 USD.

Photo Courtesy of Nick Miller

INFRACTION 167

February 14, 2010

■ ■ ■

Amount: $12 USD.

February 14, 2010 INFRACTION 168

■ ■ ■

Amount: $24 USD.

INFRACTION 169

February 20, 2010

"The Emperor has no clothes . . . and she does ***NOT*** have the body for it. Meowwwwwwww, am I right???"

■ ■ ■

Location: Oscar party.

Occasion: See-through dress on the red carpet.

Amount: $9 USD.

March 20, 2010

INFRACTION 170

"Anyone want to come to the park and play Hot Mom or Babysitter?

■ ■ ■

Location: Front door.

Occasion: First day of spring.

Amount: $5 USD.

Notes: Always guess "Mom" on Saturdays.

March 21, 2010

"Show me an unpleasant fine-dining experience, and I'll show you an off-year Cabernet."

■ ■ ■

Location: Bathroom.

Occasion: Flossing.

Amount: $18 USD.

March 23, 2010

INFRACTION 172

"Call me old-fashioned, but when it comes to porn archetypes, I'll take one sexy librarian over ten sexy bloggers."

■ ■ ■

Location: Lenscrafters.

Occasion: Chick wearing glasses.

Amount: $17 USD.

Notes:

{ turn the page }

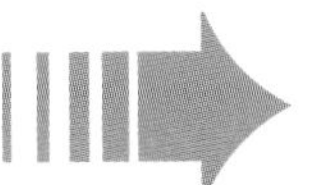

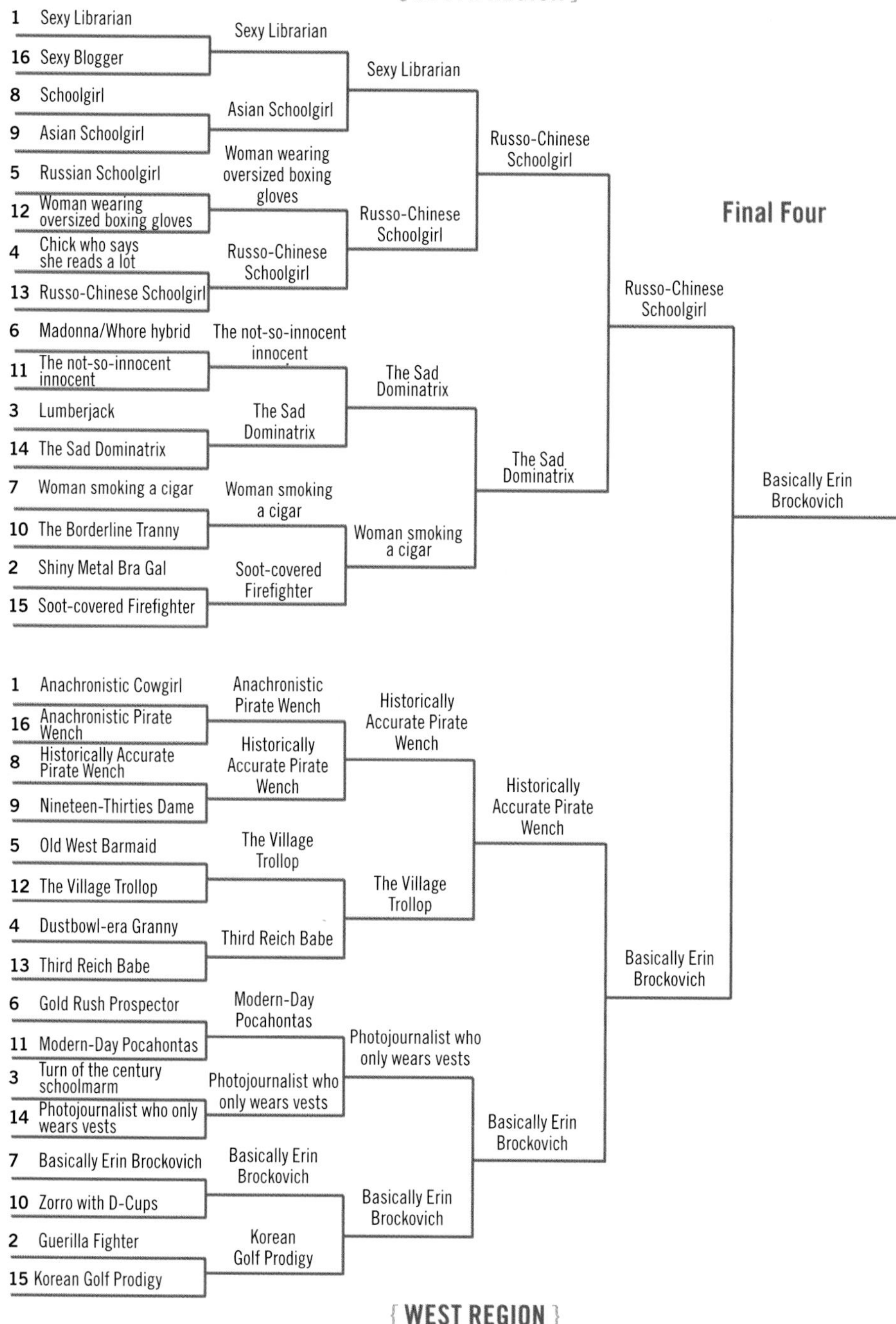
{ SOUTH REGION }
1 Sexy Librarian
16 Sexy Blogger
8 Schoolgirl
9 Asian Schoolgirl
5 Russian Schoolgirl
12 Woman wearing oversized boxing gloves
4 Chick who says she reads a lot
13 Russo-Chinese Schoolgirl
6 Madonna/Whore hybrid
11 The not-so-innocent innocent
3 Lumberjack
14 The Sad Dominatrix
7 Woman smoking a cigar
10 The Borderline Tranny
2 Shiny Metal Bra Gal
15 Soot-covered Firefighter
Sexy Librarian
Asian Schoolgirl
Woman wearing oversized boxing gloves
Russo-Chinese Schoolgirl
The not-so-innocent innocent
The Sad Dominatrix
Woman smoking a cigar
Soot-covered Firefighter
Sexy Librarian
Russo-Chinese Schoolgirl
The Sad Dominatrix
Woman smoking a cigar
Russo-Chinese Schoolgirl
The Sad Dominatrix
Russo-Chinese Schoolgirl
Final Four
Basically Erin Brockovich
1 Anachronistic Cowgirl
16 Anachronistic Pirate Wench
8 Historically Accurate Pirate Wench
9 Nineteen-Thirties Dame
5 Old West Barmaid
12 The Village Trollop
4 Dustbowl-era Granny
13 Third Reich Babe
6 Gold Rush Prospector
11 Modern-Day Pocahontas
3 Turn of the century schoolmarm
14 Photojournalist who only wears vests
7 Basically Erin Brockovich
10 Zorro with D-Cups
2 Guerilla Fighter
15 Korean Golf Prodigy
Anachronistic Pirate Wench
Historically Accurate Pirate Wench
The Village Trollop
Third Reich Babe
Modern-Day Pocahontas
Photojournalist who only wears vests
Basically Erin Brockovich
Korean Golf Prodigy
Historically Accurate Pirate Wench
The Village Trollop
Photojournalist who only wears vests
Basically Erin Brockovich
Historically Accurate Pirate Wench
Basically Erin Brockovich
Basically Erin Brockovich
{ WEST REGION }

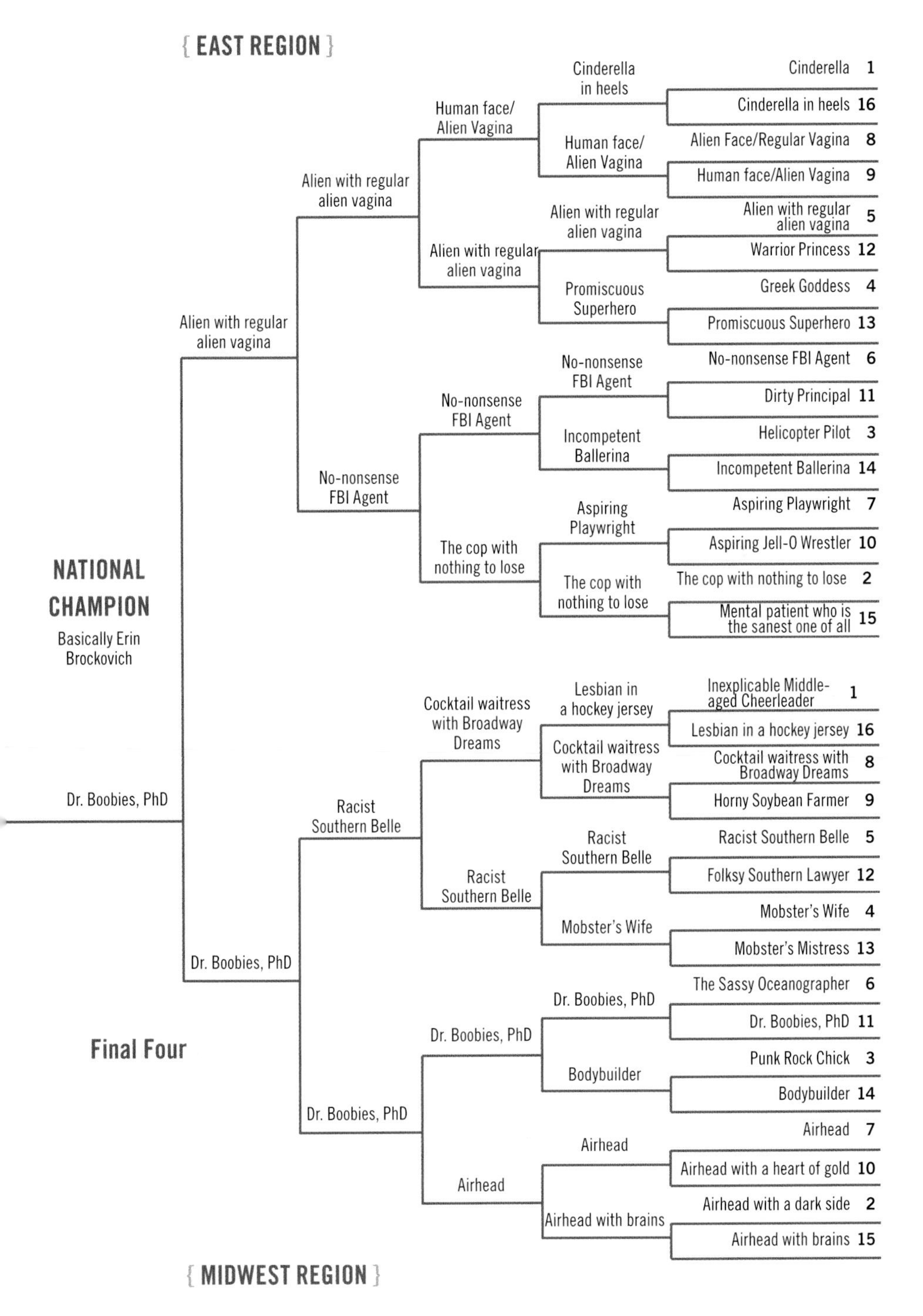

{ EAST REGION }
Cinderella 1
Cinderella in heels 16
Alien Face/Regular Vagina 8
Human face/Alien Vagina 9
Alien with regular alien vagina 5
Warrior Princess 12
Greek Goddess 4
Promiscuous Superhero 13
No-nonsense FBI Agent 6
Dirty Principal 11
Helicopter Pilot 3
Incompetent Ballerina 14
Aspiring Playwright 7
Aspiring Jell-O Wrestler 10
The cop with nothing to lose 2
Mental patient who is the sanest one of all 15
Cinderella in heels
Human face/ Alien Vagina
Alien with regular alien vagina
Promiscuous Superhero
No-nonsense FBI Agent
Incompetent Ballerina
Aspiring Playwright
The cop with nothing to lose
Human face/ Alien Vagina
Alien with regular alien vagina
No-nonsense FBI Agent
The cop with nothing to lose
Alien with regular alien vagina
No-nonsense FBI Agent
Alien with regular alien vagina
NATIONAL CHAMPION
Basically Erin Brockovich
Dr. Boobies, PhD
Inexplicable Middle-aged Cheerleader 1
Lesbian in a hockey jersey 16
Cocktail waitress with Broadway Dreams 8
Horny Soybean Farmer 9
Racist Southern Belle 5
Folksy Southern Lawyer 12
Mobster's Wife 4
Mobster's Mistress 13
The Sassy Oceanographer 6
Dr. Boobies, PhD 11
Punk Rock Chick 3
Bodybuilder 14
Airhead 7
Airhead with a heart of gold 10
Airhead with a dark side 2
Airhead with brains 15
Lesbian in a hockey jersey
Cocktail waitress with Broadway Dreams
Racist Southern Belle
Mobster's Wife
Dr. Boobies, PhD
Bodybuilder
Airhead
Airhead with brains
Cocktail waitress with Broadway Dreams
Racist Southern Belle
Dr. Boobies, PhD
Airhead
Racist Southern Belle
Dr. Boobies, PhD
Dr. Boobies, PhD
Final Four
{ MIDWEST REGION }

April 14, 2010

"Abercrombie has his moments, but Fitch is deadweight."

■ ■ ■

Location: The Grove.

Occasion: Killing time before taping of *Access Hollywood*.

Amount: $20 USD.

"Bulldogs may be hideous, but at least they also can't breathe."

■ ■ ■

Location: Animal shelter.

Occasion: Date gone awry.

Amount: $35 USD.

Notes: Honestly, we gotta let these things go. Darwin is turning over in his grave. Also: Hey pandas! I'm onto you too! Get busy screwin' or get busy dyin'.

April 27, 2010

"It would be so much easier for me to invest in *Les Misérables* if I knew what kind of bread he was stealing."

■ ■ ■

Location: Playhouse lobby.

Occasion: Intermission.

Amount: $30 USD.

Notes: If it's pumpernickel I get it. Anything else and it's like "Make it at home" you know?

"If I had to sum up my interior design philosophy in three words it would be: credenzas, credenzas, credenzas."

■ ■ ■

Location: Estate sale.

Occasion: Some guy died . . . and not from good taste.

Amount: $19 USD.

May 9, 2010

"The bartender wouldn't put a tiny straw in my cocktail if she didn't want me to use it."

■ ■ ■

Location: Bar.

Occasion: Unfair scolding.

Amount: $11 USD.

May 10, 2010

INFRACTION 178

"It's not a question of 'if' we're going to get a saltwater fish tank, it's a question of 'when.' "

■ ■ ■

Location: Long Beach Aquarium.

Occasion: Moment of connection with spotted eagle ray.

Amount: $21 USD.

INFRACTION 179 *May 11, 2010*

"If Crabtree & Evelyn is already the name of a store, then what the hell am I supposed to call my Lesbian Wild West novel?"

■ ■ ■

Location: Mall.

Occasion: Browsing.

Amount: $6 USD.

Notes:

{ Fallback Titles For My Lesbian Wild West Novel, Pending Letter From Crabtree & Evelyn's Legal Representation: }

"All Holsters, No Guns"

"Butch Cassidy & Butch Jane"

"Stirrups"

"The Woman from Bryn Mawr"

"3:10 to Santa Fe"

"They Died With Their Bras Off"

"The Indigo Squaws"

"Lonesome Dove, Well-fed Cats"

"The Treasure of the Sierra Madre-on-Madre"

"Billie the Kid Jean King"

"Wagons West, Vibrators South"

"Dances with Wendy"

"McCabe & Mrs. Miller plus Mrs. Jenkins minus McCabe"

"The Vagina Sheriff"

"The Totally *TOTALLY* Forgiven and Even Encouraged"

"A Fistful of Fisting"

"Jacoby & Meyers"

May 25, 2010

"If colored Tupperware didn't exist, I would have to invent it."

■ ■ ■

Location: Potluck dinner.

Occasion: Perfectly transported couscous.

Amount: $13 USD.

"Brunettes are your workhorses, blondes are your show horses, and redheads are unbroken and wild."

■ ■ ■

Location: Couch.

Occasion: Cinemax free preview weekend.

Amount: $4 USD.

June 3, 2010

"I'd give anything to have amethyst for a birthstone."

■ ■ ■

Location: Jewelry store.

Occasion: Window shopping.

Amount: $22 USD.

"Murder-suicide blah blah blah. Wake me up when there's a suicide-*MURDER*."

■ ■ ■

Location: Couch.

Occasion: 11 O'Clock News.

Amount: $7 USD.

Notes:

Let's get creative people!

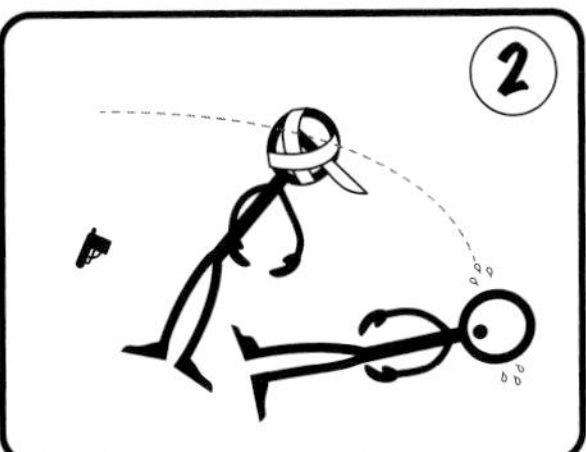

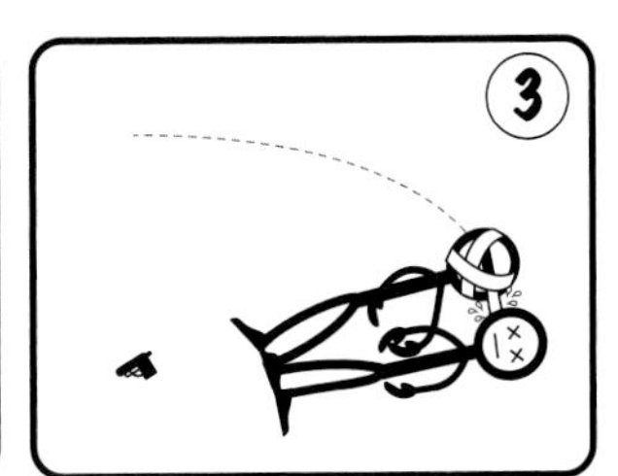

June 16, 2010

"You know what's a catchy tune? 'Stairway to Heaven.' "

■ ■ ■

Location: Bathroom.

Occasion: Getting ready for bed.

Amount: $9 USD.

"You're laughing now, but pretty soon everyone will have Transitions lenses."

■ ■ ■

Location: Hot tub.

Occasion: Summer solstice.

Amount: $6 USD.

June 30, 2010

“Never before have there been so many geniuses working in the medium of scented candle.”

■ ■ ■

Location: Pottery Barn.

Occasion: Attempted wheedling of employee discount.

Amount: $14 USD.

"If it's not a long conversation about *Inception*, I don't want to have it."

■ ■ ■

Location: Car.

Occasion: Blown mind.

Amount: $5 USD.

Notes: My totem is all five dice from a game of Yahtzee.

INFRACTION 188

August 2, 2010

"They haven't invented a problem that Zumba can't solve."

■ ■ ■

Location: Bathroom.

Occasion: Weigh-in.

Amount: $8 USD.

Notes:

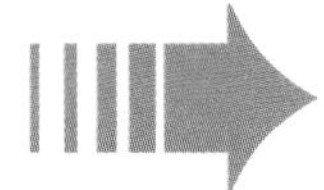

PROBLEM	SOLUTION
Racism (traditional, systemic, unintentional)	Zumba
Greed/Avarice	Zumba
Athlete's foot	Zumba
Identity theft	Zumba
Drunk Driving	Zumba
Difficulty proving/disproving God's existence	Zumba
Language barriers	Zumba
Immediate regret due to experimental menu choice	Zumba
Immediate regret due to safe menu choice	Zumba
Insomnia	Zumba
Dangerous predators (sharks, alligators, cobra snakes)	Zumba
Depreciation of currency	Zumba
Depression of world market	Zumba
Corporate influence in politics	Zumba
Moral depravity	Zumba
Feelings of hopelessness	Zumba
Drugs / Addiction	Zumba
In a world where shelf life and appearance trumps all, most produce still tastes like garbage	Zumba
Dandruff	Zumba
Folding fitted sheets	Zumba
Fear	Zumba

INFRACTION 189

August 10, 2010

"The faux-hawk is the only true game-changing haircut."

■ ■ ■

Location: Stop sign.

Occasion: Car full of weirdos.

Amount: $12 USD.

"If I had to sum up my life in one movie it would be *Eat Pray Love Sex Lies & Videotape . . . Tango & Cash.*"

■ ■ ■

Location: Funeral home.

Occasion: Grandfather's death.

Amount: $7 USD.

INFRACTION
191

September 4, 2010

"Regardless of gender, I'm naming my first child Sussudio."

■ ■ ■

Location: Plane ride.

Occasion: Brief sighting through first-class curtain of Sir Phil Collins.

Amount: $24 USD.

"More like 'Whoomp, there it's ***NOT***!' "

■ ■ ■

Location: Dance floor.

Occasion: Cousin's bat mitzvah.

Amount: $14 USD.

September 10, 2010

Photo Courtesy of Nick Miller

■ ■ ■

Amount: $17 USD.

Notes: Because it's 80 degrees out, that's why.

September 14, 2010

INFRACTION 194

"Otter say what???"

■ ■ ■

Location: SeaWorld San Diego.

Occasion: Seal & Otter Show.

Amount: $29 USD.

September 15, 2010

"I'm fluent in all the Bromance languages."

■ ■ ■

Location: Indian reservation.

Occasion: Sweat lodge.

Amount: $24 USD.

"God created spats to be worn, dammit!"

■ ■ ■

Location: Dinner table.

Occasion: Heated argument.

Amount: $11 USD.

INFRACTION 197

September 20, 2010

"Is 7.3 megapixels really enough to capture my essence?"

■ ■ ■

Location: Best Buy.

Occasion: Old video camera takes a ball gag to the lens.

Amount: $6 USD.

Notes: 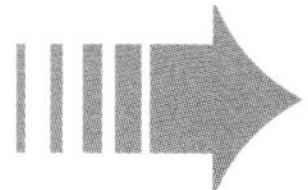

{ VARIOUS MEDIUMS: Do They Capture My Essence? }

MEDIUM	YES	NO
Oil		X
Tempera		X
Tempura		X
Acrylic		X
Pen and ink		X
Performance art		X
Fresco		X
Loom tapestry		X
Wax sculpture		X
En plein air watercolor		X
Frieze		X
Mobile		X
Charcoal		X
Totem pole		X
Jazz		X
Classical bust		X
Mosaic		X
Sumi		X
Human chess board	X	
Papier-macheâ		X
Salvaged copper		X
Street art		X
Video installation		X
Chalk		X
Ice sculpture		X
Colored sand		X

INFRACTION **198** *September 21, 2010*

"If Mexico is anything like Señor Frog's Myrtle Beach, I'm going to retire there."

■ ■ ■

Location: Merrill Lynch.

Occasion: Meeting with financial planner.

Amount: $19 USD.

"My perfect woman has Lady Mary's looks and Lady Edith's self-esteem."

■ ■ ■

Location: Couch.

Occasion: *Downton Abbey* British premiere.

Amount: $12 USD.

INFRACTION 200

September 28, 2010

"It's so hot outside you can hear old people dying."

■ ■ ■

Location: Front door.

Occasion: Heat wave.

Amount: $10 USD.

"Hold everything. The Most Interesting Man in the World and the Men's Wearhouse guy are two different people???"

■ ■ ■

Location: Dinner Table.

Occasion: Bona fide *Beautiful Mind* moment.

Amount: $8 USD.

Photo Courtesy of Nick Miller

INFRACTION 202

October 25, 2010

"I need another full-length mirror in my room if I'm going to accurately assess the tautness of my hammies."

■ ■ ■

Location: Bed, Bath & Beyond.

Occasion: Mirror shopping.

Amount: $24 USD.

Notes: Naming one's muscles has to be earned . . .

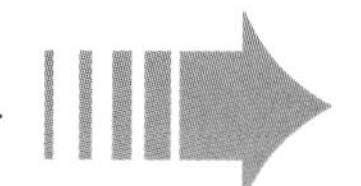

MUSCLE AREA	NAME	HAVE I EARNED IT?	
		"Not Quite Yet"	"Hell Yes, Bro!"
Left shoulder	Deltoid Burke		X
Right shoulder	Rookie of the Year		X
Right leg	The Quad City DJs	X	
Left leg	American Messi		X
Neck	Dr. Trapezius Arbuckle	X	
Hips	The Flexor Sisters	X	
Stomach	The Township of Washboard Glen		X
Obliques	The Ab-dominal Snowmen	X	
Back	The "Lats" Word with Lawrence O'Donnell		X
Biceps	The Bi-Curious Strongmen	X	
Chest	The Aurora Pectoralis	X	
Glutes	Vice City		X

INFRACTION 203

October 30, 2010

"It's a fob chain, you monsters. Or would you have me leave my pocket watch unattached to my waistcoat?"

■ ■ ■

Location: Halloween party.

Occasion: Sherlock Holmes: The Costume.

Amount: $15 USD.

Notes: I found Jude Law's portrayal of Doctor Watson to be riveting, but Robert Downey Jr.'s Holmes to be coarse.

DOUCHEBAG
JAR

ACKNOWLEDGEMENTS

Throughout the writing of this book, as throughout life, I had and have but one true compass: the undying wisdom, patience, and inspiration so generously provided by the following people, places, and things:

Mom, Nana, Wu-Tang, Aunt Debbie, Ethan Allen, fancy ginger ale, the people of Ciudad Juárez Mexico, NASA, Hu Jintao, our brave men and women in uniform, Invisalign, Tupac, Hammer, Flea, my natural curiosity, Thesaurus.com, that guy at Key Club everyone calls Toothpick, gumption, earnestness, awe, the American steelworker, Cross-Fit, high-quality orthotics, Jessica Lange's timeless countenance, fat beats, The estate of Erica Peterson, citrus, Daylight Savings, low-fat custard, Dr. Gideon Morales D.D.S., Fiat, 260 GSM paper, meditation, karate, anyone who ever said "Schmidt, I can't begin to process the bone-chillingly deep shit you're saying at this specific moment—write it down, man . . . *write it down*," ham, backlit keyboards, success, bicentennial coins, the fat kid who played Jamie on *Small Wonder*, the surviving members of Heart, Flannery O'Connor, Christmas, RU-83 in theory, Ed Bradley's chutzpah, John Negroponte, The Woz, our national parks, autumn, T-9, *Cujo*-era Stephen King, *The Relentless Pursuit of Sinew* exercise DVD series, IATSE

Local 11, our forefathers, Silicon Valley, *House of Buggin'* night at The Leguizarium, pure jojoba extract, River Phoenix RIP, sunsets, children, courage in the workplace, The James L. Knight Foundation, "Dreams of my Father," Entenmann's, the work ethic of the Japanese, Procter & Gamble, Breathe-Right nasal strips, the best husband/wife Pilates instructing team on the planet you know who you are, my old humidifier, Calvin Klein fitted Ts, gourmet pancakes outdoors at dusk, The Cloud, custom-made Steve Madden Heelys, the razor-sharp wit of Doris Kearns Goodwin, WordPerfect for Windows, The Nevada Gaming Commission, Unicef, Stacy Keach, The Platters, wainscoting that takes a chance, teak, Mrs. Sophia Lear-Samo CPA, both *Trons*, Alaska Airlines, Knott's Berry Farm, Knott's Scary Farm, Strunk & White, Tempurpedic mattress technology, Farm Aid, the Brady Bill, pocket doors, show dogs, Sub-Zero appliances, the solution to Wednesday's jumble, erotic topiary, properly cared for silver, Tavis Smiley, the breathtaking symmetry of pinecones, free diving, loose-leaf tea, *Johnny Mnemonic*, whistle-blowers with hungry mouths to feed who still choose to risk everything, kumquats, Jennifer Schuster and alllllll my crazy muthafuckas at Harp-to-the-Collzzz, Nick, Winston, Coach, sugar-free applesauce, and The RAND Corporation.

ABOUT THE AUTHOR

Mr. Schmidt is a one-time lecturer at The Learning Annex, and the author of the self-published Young Adult novel "Babysitting, Babysat." He lives in Los Angeles, California with three roommates.

ABOUT THE TYPEFACE

Everything but Wingdings, bitches!!!